TOM BITES BACK

MIDDLE SCHOOL BITES

TOM BITES BACK

BY

Steven Banks

ILLUSTRATED BY Mark Fearing

HOLIDAY HOUSE ❖ New York

HOLIDAY HOUSE is registered in the U.S. Patent and Trademark Office.

Printed and bound in June 2020 at Toppan Leefung, DongGuan City, China.

www.holidayhouse.com

First Edition

1 3 5 7 9 10 8 6 4 2

Library of Congress Cataloging-in-Publication Data

Names: Banks, Steven, 1954- author. | Fearing, Mark, illustrator.

Title: Tom bites back / by Steven Banks ; illustrated by Mark Fearing.

Description: First edition. | New York : Holiday House, [2020] |

Series: Middle school bites ; #2 | Audience: Ages 8-12. | Audience: Grades 4-6.

Summary: Eleven-year-old Tom the Vam-Wolf-Zom meets Martha, the

244-year-old vampire who bit him, and convinces her to teach him such

important things as how to fly and how to hypnotize people.

Identifiers: LCCN 2019055025 | ISBN 9780823446155 (hardcover)

Subjects: CYAC: Middle schools—Fiction. | Schools—Fiction. |

Vampires—Fiction. | Werewolves—Fiction. | Zombies—Fiction. | Humorous

stories.

Classification: LCC PZ7.B22637 Tom 2020 | DDC [Fic]—dc23

LC record available at https://lccn.loc.gov/2019055025

To my sons, James and Spencer,
who know the importance of family,
friends, and a good Halloween
costume, and who have brought
me immeasurable joy.

1.

The Bat That Spoke

The bat on the windowsill looked up and said, "Hello?"

I wasn't surprised that a bat was talking to me. A lot of weird and crazy stuff had happened that week.

1. The day before I started middle school, I got bit by a vampire bat. (When I was asleep, but I thought it was just a spider bite.)

2. Then I got bit by a werewolf. (When I was running, but I thought it was just a big dog.)

3. After that, I got bit by a zombie. (When I went into an old carnival trailer at a creepy gas station, but I thought it was fake.)

4. I turned into a Vam-Wolf-Zom.

5. I told my best friend, Zeke, and we found out I have super hearing, night vision, and awesome strength and speed. But I can't turn into a bat and fly, which is totally unfair.

6. I found out that I'll live forever, unless the sun burns me up or I get a wooden stake in the heart or shot by a silver bullet or if somebody chops my head off. (I guess everybody dies if they get their head chopped off.)

7. Emma, The Worst Sister in the World, found out I was a Vam-Wolf-Zom when she saw me drinking blood from a raw steak. She told our parents.

8. My parents decided I should tell everybody at a school assembly, where the principal announced they had to treat me like a normal kid.

9. I got suspended for a day because I threatened to rip somebody's throat out. (I only said it to scare him, so he wouldn't beat up this kid named Abel Sherrill.)

After The Worst First Week of Middle School Ever, my family went up to my gram's house in the woods for the weekend, where I got all my bites.

The night we got there we had a big dinner of barbecued spareribs. I have to eat a lot because I'm one-third zombie. Zombies aren't hungry 24-7 like on TV, but when you get hungry, you are REALLY hungry.

There was a full moon that night, so I turned into a werewolf. Gram hadn't seen me do that yet. She thought I made a good werewolf; she loves old horror movies and we usually watch them when we visit her. But that night, Emma picked a stupid, boring, romantic movie. When it was over, I went up to bed, and that's when the bat appeared on my windowsill.

I just sort of stood there, staring at it.

"*Hello?*" it said again, louder. "Bonjour? . . . Hola? . . . Guten Nacht? . . . Ciao? . . . Namaste? . . . Marhaba? . . . Ohayo?"

It sounded like a girl bat.

"Hi . . ." I said.

"Well, that is most fortunate," said the bat. "You can speak. This shall be a more interesting conversation."

She talked like Abel Sherrill, The Second-Weirdest Kid at My School. (I'm the first.) He wears a suit and tie to school every single day and carries a briefcase. We share a locker. It bugged me at first, but now I don't mind so much.

"Are . . . are you the bat that bit me last week?" I asked.

"Yes. That would be me."

I wanted to smash her. If this stupid bat hadn't bitten me, I wouldn't be a vampire. Or one-third vampire. But I also wanted to ask a million questions, so I didn't smash her.

The bat looked me up and down. "I did not

know you were a werewolf. You certainly didn't taste like one."

I forgot I was in full werewolf mode. I guess I was getting used to the hair.

"The werewolf bit me *after* you did," I said. "Why'd you have to bite me anyway?"

"Are you a dunderhead?"

I didn't know what a dunderhead was, but it didn't sound like a compliment.

"What do you mean?" I asked.

"I am a vampire. That is what we do. I was flying by and needed blood. The old woman's window was closed, unfortunately—"

"That's Gram, this is her house."

"—and your window was open."

"Why'd you have to turn me into a vampire?"

"I assure you, lad, that was not my intention. It was an accident."

"How can you accidentally turn somebody into a vampire?"

"I had bitten you and was preparing to drink, but let me make this perfectly clear, this has *never* happened before, because *you* moved and tried to swat me, I bit my lip. A drop of my blood dripped into the bite I had made on your neck. Once a vampire's blood mixes with a human's, they will turn. As you did."

"I'm a vampire because you bit your lip?!"

"Precisely. Consider yourself lucky. If I had drunk all your blood, we would not be having this conversation."

She looked past me, into the room. "Are you alone here?"

"No. My parents and sister and Gram are here—"

I had a horrible thought. *She wanted to suck their blood.* In a split second I grabbed the bat and held her in my fist. I can move super fast when I want to. That's one good thing about being part vampire and part werewolf. Zombies are major slowpokes. There is nothing good about being a zombie.

The bat squirmed and wiggled and tried to get free.

"Unhand me this instant!"

"Don't bite anybody here!"

"Let me go!"

"Not until you say you won't bite anybody."

I squeezed her a little to show I was serious. I didn't want her accidentally turning Mom, Dad, Gram, Emma, or our dog, Muffin, into vampires. Are there vampire dogs?

"Very well," she said. "I shall not bite anyone."

"No! You have to say, 'I swear on blood'!" I said, holding her a few inches from my face.

She gave me a disgusted look.

"I swear on blood I shall not bite anyone in this house. Now put me down, you ninnyhammer!"

Ninnyhammer didn't sound good either.

I set her back down on the windowsill. Now I knew I could trust her. Last week Zeke said that if a vampire swears a blood oath it was binding. If they went back on their promise they melted or disintegrated or burst into flames or something.

"I've got a zillion questions," I said.

"I shall answer a few and then I must be on my way."

The bat flew farther into the room, whizzing right by my ear, and landed on my pillow. I wasn't thrilled she was on my pillow. I mean, bats are kind of like rats with wings.

"First, I have a question for *you*, lad," she said. "How did you become a werewolf?"

"A werewolf bit me when I was running," I said, sitting down in a chair. "But, I'm only one-third werewolf."

"One-third? Pray tell, how is that so?"

I told her about getting bit by the zombie.

"You are also part zombie?" she said, her little bat eyes getting big.

"Yeah. I'm a Vam-Wolf-Zom."

She nodded. "Vam-Wolf-Zom. . . . Very clever.

I am naturally fond of vampires, on the whole; I tolerate werewolves; but zombies are another matter. Good for nothing, brainless eating machines."

Nobody likes zombies. Except maybe other zombies. Gram loves zombie movies, but it's not the same.

The bat walked toward me, across my pillow, leaving little bat foot imprints. She looked up at my face. "Absolutely fascinating. In all my two hundred and forty-four years, I have never chanced upon nor heard of such a creature."

"Never? I'm the only one— Wait! You're two hundred and forty-four years old?!"

Knock! Knock! Knock!

Someone was outside my door.

2.

Calling the White House

I t was my sister, Emma. I know her knock. She always uses her fist and bangs on the door as hard as she can.

The bat dove under my pillow. I really hoped she didn't have fleas.

"Hey! Freakazoid!" Emma yelled.

Freakazoid was Emma's latest nickname for me. Ever since I became a Vam-Wolf-Zom she'd called me a lot of different names. I think she was trying them out before she settled on the best one. So far she had called me:

It
Bitey
Monster Boy
Creepy
Creepazoid
Creep Freak
Gruesome
Terrible Tom
Mutant
Disgusting Boy
He Who Shall
Not Be Normal

"Who are you talking to?" yelled Emma from the other side of the door.

"Zeke!" I yelled back. "I called him to ask about some history homework."

Emma would go ballistic if she knew the vampire bat that had bitten me was in my room. She'd probably call the police, the FBI, and a SWAT team. I bet she'd call the White House.

"Hello. This is the White House. How may I help you?"

"This is Emma Marks! The vampire bat that bit my brother is in my grandmother's house! Send the army and navy and marines over! You need to declare war!"

"I'm sorry, we can't do that. Only Congress can declare war."

"Are you serious?!"

"Yes. You should have learned that in school. What grade did you get in Government class?"

"I probably got an A. You have to get rid of this bat!"

"Let me bring your report card up on my computer . . . You got a C."

"Are you going to help me with this vampire bat or not?"

"Would you like me to connect you to The Federal Bureau of Vampire Bat Task Force Operations?"

"Yes! I would! It's about time!"

"I'm joking, Ms. Marks. There is no such organization."

"That is NOT funny!"

I could totally see Emma doing that.

"Did you steal my toothpaste?!" she yelled, from the hallway.

"No!"

"Yes, you did!"

"No, I didn't!"

"Let me come in and see for sure!"

Emma uses toothpaste that supposedly makes your teeth super white and bright. She's always smiling at herself in the mirror. She had braces until a year ago and complained about them every single day. I guess I might have to get braces since I have fangs now.

"I don't have your stupid toothpaste, Emma!"

Emma made a noise that sounded like a bear growling. Then she stomped down the hall. I locked my door, turned back around, and there was a girl staring at me.

3.

The 244-Year-Old Girl

It was just like a horror movie, when a creepy-looking girl climbs out of a well or suddenly appears in a mirror.

She looked about thirteen or fourteen. She was thin and a little taller than me, with long, red hair that went down her back, green eyes, and a pale, white face. She was wearing a dark green dress that looked like she was going to a Halloween party or a funeral.

"Who are you?" I asked.

"Martha Livingston, of Philadelphia, Pennsylvania."

She held up the two sides of her dress with her fingers, bowed her head a little, and curtsied. I wasn't sure what I was supposed to do, so I bowed back. Did I have to learn vampire manners? I didn't know what to say. I'd just been talking to a bat, and now the bat was a girl.

"And what is your name, lad? It is customary to introduce oneself."

"Oh. I'm Thomas Marks." I don't know why I said "Thomas" instead of "Tom." "Are you really two hundred and forty-four years old?" I asked.

"Let me clarify: I have existed on the earth for that long. I was thirteen when I was turned." She looked like a girl, but she sounded like a grown-up. It was easier talking to a girl than a bat.

I didn't want Mom, Dad, Gram, or Emma to hear us talking, so I turned on an old radio that Gram keeps on the desk in the room. Some boring classical music with pianos and violins playing the same thing over and over came on.

Martha closed her eyes and smiled. "Mozart's twenty-first piano concerto in C major. I heard him play that in the Burgtheater in Vienna, 1785."

I didn't know what she was talking about, so I just nodded.

She opened her eyes and said, "Who was the shrieking female at the door?"

"That's my sister, Emma."

"She is high-spirited."

"She's a major pain in the butt."

"How did you know about the blood oath, Thomas?"

"My best friend Zeke told me."

"He must be a wise and learned fellow."

Zeke was sort of the opposite of a wise and learned fellow. But he did know a lot of stuff about monsters. He would love to meet Martha.

"Is he a true, loyal, and honest friend?" she asked.

"He is."

"You are lucky. As Benjamin Franklin said, 'A true friend is the best possession.' You have other friends too?"

"Yeah. There's this girl named Annie Barstow and a guy named Abel Sherrill—he's a new friend."

"Annie Barstow is someone you are fond of? Your girlfriend, perhaps?"

Why do people *always* ask that when you say you have a friend that's a girl?

"No. She's just a friend."

Martha sat down in an old rocking chair in the corner of the room and folded her hands in her lap. "Since you will not allow me to feed, our time here must be brief. What do you wish to ask of me?"

"Can you teach me how to turn into a bat and fly?"

"No. I cannot."

"Oh, come on! You gotta teach me!"

She raised an eyebrow. "Oh, really? I do? And where exactly does it say I am to be your personal vampire instructor?"

"It's your fault I'm a vampire! Everybody at school keeps asking me, 'Can you turn into a bat and fly?'"

"Teaching transformation and flying takes time, which I do not have this evening. Let us get to the important matters at hand. Fetch paper and pen, so you may take notes."

I grabbed some notebook paper and a pen from my backpack and sat at the desk chair.

"Choose your victims carefully," she said, rocking back and forth. "Make sure you are alone when you feed. No public spaces. Caves are excellent; dark alleys, abandoned buildings, the woods, a secluded park—"

"But wait, I don't—"

"Shush! Do not attack. Either persuade or charm the victim. The jugular vein is best. Steady the victim's neck or skull. Pierce the skin with your fangs. They will usually faint, so be prepared to catch them. Feed quickly, but efficiently. Do not make a pig of yourself. Cease when full."

"Whoa, whoa, whoa! I don't want to suck anybody's blood!"

She stopped rocking in the chair. "Good heavens, lad, you must feed or you will surely die."

"No way. It's too gross."

Martha shook her head and sighed. "One of *those*, are you? You're as bad as vegetarians. Where have you been getting your blood?"

"I get it from uncooked meat."

She scrunched up her face. "How pathetic."

"And they have a synthetic blood you can buy."

"I tried it . . . once. Never again. It's as bad as Diet Coke. How often do you feed?"

"Every three or four days. I guess I don't need blood as much as you do, because I'm only one-third vampire."

She stood up. "Then why am I wasting my time giving you this valuable, hard-won knowledge?"

"Wait . . ." I didn't want to ask her the next question, but I had to. "Um . . . so . . . do you really *kill* people?"

"No," she snapped. "I do not kill. I am what is known as a catch-and-release vampire."

"I've never heard of that," I said doubtfully.

"Well, *I* had never heard of a Vam-Wolf-Zom, but one exists, does it not? I only suck enough blood to quench my thirst. I leave the person, or animal, light-headed, weakened, with a small scar, but they recover."

She walked toward the desk and looked at all the homework I had to do over the weekend. I couldn't believe how much homework we got the very first week of school. That should be illegal.

Martha picked up my U.S. history book. On the cover it had a painting of those guys who signed the Declaration of Independence. I had to write a report called *My Favorite American* for History class on Monday. I hadn't started it yet. I was trying to figure out who would be the easiest person.

Martha looked at the picture and shook her head. "That does not resemble Dr. Franklin in the least." She tossed the book down on the desk.

"How'd you become a vampire?" I asked. "Did a bat bite you?"

She sat down on the edge of the desk. "No. I was orphaned at the age of thirteen. My father died at the Battle of Concord, in 1775, my mother of the pox, a month later. A couple took me in and put me to work at the City Tavern in Philadelphia. I was a serving girl. One evening, as we were closing, I noticed that Benjamin Franklin had left his spectacles on a table. I ran outside—"

"Did you say *Benjamin Franklin*?"

"Yes."

"The guy who invented glasses and electricity?!"

Martha rolled her eyes. "Dr. Franklin did not invent glasses, he invented *bifocals*. And he did not *invent* electricity. He flew a kite with a key on a string, during a thunderstorm, to demonstrate that lightning *was* electricity."

"You actually knew Benjamin Franklin?!"

"Yes! May I finish my tale, please? Dr. Franklin was a brisk walker and quite tall, so I had to run like the devil to catch up with him. I called out, he turned around and—"

"Ben Franklin bit you?! Ben Franklin was a vampire!"

I couldn't wait to tell Zeke. He would go crazy.

"No!" said Martha.

She gave me the same kind of dirty look that Emma gives me all the time. "Stop interrupting me! Good Lord, lad, you are trying my patience. Dr. Franklin was *not* a vampire."

Zeke would be really disappointed. I was too.

"I returned his spectacles to him, he doffed his hat and said, 'Many thanks, my dear Martha. I should heed my own advice: Haste does indeed make waste.' Then he placed two pence in my hand."

"Two pennies? That's all?"

"I earned ten pence a week. Dr. Franklin was a generous tipper. I needed to make haste back

to the tavern, for I knew my master and mistress would be displeased to find me gone. I took a shortcut through an alley, which would prove to be a cataclysmic mistake. From the darkness sprang a tall, pale-faced man, with black hair and beard, wearing a long, red cloak. He grabbed me roughly about the neck. I screamed for help. Dr. Franklin came running and tried to beat the man off with his walking stick, but the man was strong. He grabbed Dr. Franklin's stick and struck him a mighty blow across the head, knocking him senseless. I tried to scream again, but the man clasped his cold, bony hand over my mouth. He dragged me through a doorway into a damp, dark room that smelled of animal hide. He bit my throat, began to drink my blood, and . . . turned me."

"Who was he?" I asked.

She took a deep breath and then let it out.

"His name was Lovick Zabrecky. I was part of his brood, for a brief time. There were four of us. I learned their ways, the rules of the nightwalkers, and then I departed. Most of my life has been spent on my own, which I prefer. For over two centuries I have stayed out of the sun's lethal rays, avoided being beheaded or burnt, escaped many an angry mob, and protected my heart from wooden stakes. There have been some close calls. But it makes life interesting, yes?"

I remembered something. "Hey! I have to do a report for my History class called *My Favorite American*. Can you tell me more stuff about Ben Franklin?"

"I am not here to help you with your schoolwork, lad. What other questions do you have? Quickly now."

She was not exactly the most patient vampire. Were they all like this?

"How am I ever going to learn to turn into a bat and fly if you won't teach me?"

"There are a few books on the subject."

"Can I get them on the Internet?"

"No," she scoffed. "They are rare, expensive, and quite difficult to obtain, though not impossible. You may also, perchance, run into another vampire who will teach you."

"Are there a lot of other vampires around?"

"Very few."

"Are they all like you?" That didn't come out right.

She got offended. "Of course not! Just like people, no two vampires are alike. Different personalities, different breeds and strains. Some can stand a bit of sunlight, if protected. I, alas, cannot take a single beam. I would go up like a torch."

"I can go out in the sun as long as I put on sunscreen and wear sunglasses, and a hat, and clothes that cover my skin."

"That proves my point, Thomas Marks. Some vampires can transform into other creatures, some cannot—"

"Wait. You mean I might *not* be able to turn into a bat and fly?"

"Precisely."

That was the only good thing about being a vampire. If I couldn't fly, that would really suck.

Martha went on. "Some of us can turn into mist, fog, or smoke."

Zeke hadn't told me that.

"Which allows one to disappear, to escape, to observe people and go unnoticed. To slip through small spaces: under a door, through a window crack. It allows one to go almost anywhere. However, it is not easily learned and can be dangerous."

Knock, knock, knock.

That wasn't Emma's knock.

4.

Questions and Answers

Gram was knocking on the door.

"Tommy?"

"Yeah?"

"It's getting late, I think it's time to turn off the music and hit the hay."

"Oh. Okay, Gram, I will. 'Night."

"'Night, Tommy."

I listened to her footsteps go down the hall and heard her door close.

"I must depart," said Martha. "Farewell."

"No! Wait," I whispered. I went over to

the radio and turned it off. "Can we go down to the basement? Please? Just for like, fifteen minutes?"

I could tell she was trying to decide whether to stay longer.

"Very well, Thomas. I shall stay for fifteen minutes. No more."

Could I convince her to teach me how to fly in fifteen minutes? I had to try.

"Maybe you'd better turn back into a bat first, before we go downstairs."

Just like that, a bat was hovering by the door. I put my hoodie on. Martha the Bat flew into my hand. I carefully put her in the pocket of my hoodie before opening the door and making sure nobody was in the hallway.

As I quietly tiptoed down the hall toward the stairs, Emma's door swung open.

"What are you doing, Creepy?"

"Nothing," I said, hoping she wouldn't notice the bulge in my hoodie pocket.

"Where are you going?"

"Downstairs."

"Why?" she said, crossing her arms and leaning against the side of the door.

"I'm . . . I'm going to get more spareribs. I'm hungry."

"You are such a total zombie. Why were you listening to classical music?"

"I . . . I like it."

"No, you don't!"

"Yes, I do!"

"Since when?"

"Since tonight."

Emma looked down. "What's in your pocket?"

"Nothing." I put my hand in the pocket. I could

feel Martha. I mean the bat, which, I guess, was also Martha.

"There's something in there," said Emma.

I let out a big sigh. "Okay. . . . It's the vampire bat that bit me and I'm going to run away with it and join a vampire coven and suck people's blood and terrorize the world."

Emma opened her mouth, but she couldn't think of anything to say, which doesn't happen very often. Finally she said, "Good!" and closed her door.

Sometimes you can tell people exactly what you don't want them to know and they think you're joking.

◦ ◦ ◦

When we got down to the basement, I took Martha the Bat out of my pocket and she turned back into Martha the Girl. Gram's basement has a big sofa, a beanbag chair, old hippie posters on the wall, and a Ping-Pong table that Emma and I used to cover with blankets to make forts.

Martha sat down in the beanbag chair and smiled. "I have not sat upon one of these since 1969."

Her fangs were super white. I wish I knew what my fangs looked like, but I can't see my reflection.

"How do you keep your fangs so white?" I asked.

"I brush after every feeding and I floss. One must keep up one's appearance."

She looked down at her dress and picked off a piece of lint.

"Martha, what happens to your clothes when you turn into your bat? When you got here, you

were a bat. Then, you turned into a girl, with clothes on. Do your clothes disappear or what?"

"A vampire's clothes are actually cloaking devices, so they are invisible, in the reflective dimension, when the vampire transforms into a bat or other form."

"Oh. I get it," I said, slowly nodding my head up and down.

I had no idea what she was talking about.

"Do you live around here?" I asked.

"Temporarily."

"Hey, do you know the werewolf that bit me?"

"I do not associate with werewolves. But I'm acquainted with a few. Describe him."

"He was really big and had a gray face and white fur."

"Good Lord, lad, that is the description of a thousand wolves!"

"He had a dark circle around one eye."

Her face got serious. "Were the eyes a vivid, intense blue?"

"Yeah." I remembered seeing his blue eyes when I turned around, just before he bit me.

"That is a werewolf by the name of Darcourt. He is not to be trusted."

Why would I trust him? He bit me.

"He is dangerous and powerful. If perchance you see him again, get away as fast as you can. Unless you wish to fight him to the death."

I didn't plan to get in any fights to the death with werewolves if I could help it. I decided to change the subject. "So, what have you done for the past two hundred years?"

"I am not here to tell you my life story, Thomas Marks."

"You didn't have to go to school, did you?"

"No. I didn't. I couldn't. However, I had no wish to be a dunderhead. I snuck into libraries at night, after they closed. I have read every great work of literature. I speak and write eight different languages and play eleven musical instruments. . . . Music is my true love and passion."

She had an expression on her face like Annie gets when she talks about a great book she read, or like my mom gets when she talks about Emma and me when we were babies, or like Zeke when he talks about banjos. Sometimes I wish I felt that way about something.

"I was lucky enough to see Beethoven premiere his Ninth Symphony in Vienna—when he was completely deaf, mind you. I saw the great jazz musician Louis Armstrong play his trumpet and sing 'Potato Head Blues' on a Mississippi riverboat in New Orleans. I saw the folk singer Bob Dylan play his very first show in New York City."

Gram *loved* Bob Dylan. He was an old guy from the sixties. She plays his records all the time. His voice sounds raspy and hoarse, like he has a bad cold. In my opinion, I have a much better voice than Bob Dylan. Singing is one thing I'm okay at. That's why Annie asked me to be in her band.

"Martha, do you want to meet Gram? She'd love to talk to you."

"No!" she said sternly. "You must make a blood oath that you will tell no one about me."

I raised my hand. "I swear on blood; I won't tell Gram—"

"*Anyone!*" she said, pointing her finger at me.

"I swear on blood; I won't tell *anyone* about you."

"And mark me well, Thomas Marks: If you ever break that oath . . . you will instantly ignite into flames and burn."

I definitely didn't want to do that.

She stood up and opened the small window near the ceiling. "And now, I must depart." She wrapped her arms around herself.

"No! Wait!"

"Now what?"

"Can't you *please* teach me how to turn into a bat and fly?"

"How many times must I say no?"

"Oh, c'mon! The vampire guy that turned you, that, that Shovic Labrescky guy, he taught you stuff."

"His name is *Lovick Zabrecky.*"

"Okay, he taught you, so you gotta teach me! What about . . . what about The Code of the Vampires?"

I made that up. I didn't know if there really was a Code of the Vampires, but it sounded good. There might be.

She sneered. "There is no such thing as The Code of the Vampires."

"Well, there should be! You turned me; you should teach me!"

She crossed her arms and looked at me for a long time.

"Very well, Thomas Marks, I shall instruct you. But, do not expect to learn how to transform and fly properly all in one evening, 'tis not an easy skill. Firstly, cross your arms across your chest, palms down, fingers spread apart."

I crossed my arms like people do when they're in a coffin.

"Wait. Do you think because I'm only one-third vampire, I might be only one-third bat and the rest of me will still be human?"

"There is but one way to find out. Close your eyes."

I did.

"Now you say, 'Turn to bat. Bat, I shall be.'"

"And then what?"

"And then you shall transform."

I opened my eyes. "Really? That's *it*?"

"Yes."

"That's crazy."

"Then say it not! And do not become a bat and fly! And I shall waste my time no longer here!"

She moved toward the window.

"Wait-wait-wait! Okay, okay! I'll say it."

Why did I have to get The World's Grumpiest Vampire Teacher? Why didn't I get a nice, patient one?

Martha stared at me intently with her green eyes. "And take heed, Thomas, when you say it, believe it."

I closed my eyes, took a deep breath, and said, "Turn to bat. . . . Bat, I shall be."

5.

The Flight of the Vam-Wolf-Zom

I felt a little breeze. I opened my eyes. The room was ginormous.

The sofa looked as big as a house. The Ping-Pong table was gigantic. The beanbag chair was humongous. Martha towered over me like a giant.

"Am I a bat?" I yelled up at her.

She crouched down and peered at me. "In a manner of speaking. Let us say you are a bat, though a somewhat wolfish-looking bat, due to your werewolf state."

I held up what I thought would be my arm and

looked at it. It was a black-gray wing that I could see through. Inside the wing was what looked like a skinny arm, with three fingers and a thumb at the end. I looked down at my two tiny, claw-like, five-toed feet. I felt my ears, and they were huge in comparison to my head. I guess I was a bat.

"Let us proceed," she said. "Hold your wings straight out, shoulder height, and flap them."

I moved my arms—I mean my wings—up and down. "Like this?"

"No! Nothing like that. I shall show you." She crossed her arms and said, "Turn to bat. Bat, I shall be."

She transformed. We stood on the floor, bat face to bat face.

"Flap your wings together, in a quick, steady rhythm. Like this." She moved her wings up and down, and slowly lifted up off the ground.

I flapped my wings.

"Nothing's happening," I said. "It's not working. I can't fly."

"Beat your wings faster, lad."

I did.

I slowly lifted up off the floor and rose into the air, higher and higher.

I was flying!

It was incredible! I started beating my wings faster. It was the most unbelievable, amazing, awesome feeling ever!

It was better than Christmas, my birthday, Halloween, and a trip to Disney World combined.

"I'm flying!" I yelled as I kept going upward.

"Indeed you are," said Martha. "You are also about to crash into the ceiling."

BAM!

I crashed my head on the ceiling. I grabbed my head with both my wings, which isn't the smartest thing to do when you're supposed to be flapping them to fly. I fell straight down and crashed on the floor. I looked up to see Martha hovering over me, with a smirk on her face.

"As Dr. Franklin said, 'Pride cometh before a fall.'"

I rubbed the top of my head with my wing. "That really hurt."

"May I suggest you always look in the direction in which you are flying?"

I got up, flapped my wings, and rose back up in

the air, toward Martha. I beat my wings just fast enough so I hovered next to her.

"Now what do I do?"

"To propel yourself forward, tilt your wings down, ever so slightly."

I did it and it worked. It was amazing, until I realized I was headed straight toward the wall.

"How do I turn?!"

"Tilt slightly to the left!" she shouted.

I did, but I turned upside down and started spinning.

"I said *slightly,* Thomas!"

I kept flapping my wings and righted myself. I was a little dizzy, but I started to fly in a circle around the room.

"Okay . . . I got it. . . . Let's go outside!" I said as I flew toward the open window.

"No!" Martha followed me to the window and blocked me from going out.

"Why not?" I said as I turned to avoid her, slammed into the wall, and crash-landed on the floor.

Martha looked down and grinned. "That is one reason. You are not ready." She landed next to me. "Flying in a room is quite different from flying outside, where you must deal with winds, air currents, temperature, and . . . predators."

I didn't like the sound of that. "Predators?"

"Hawks and owls that *love* to eat tasty little bats. Watch for owls—they make no noise when they fly."

I hadn't thought about getting eaten.

"And when you are on the ground, or in a tree or a cave, watch out for snakes, weasels, and raccoons. Small birds may fly into a bat cave when you are sleeping and peck you to death."

I decided I was NEVER going to go to sleep when I was a bat.

"Also, take care when flying over rivers and lakes, as fish have been known to leap up and take down a bat."

Why is everything not as great as you imagine it's going to be? There's always something that wrecks it.

"What happens if something eats me when I'm a bat?" I asked.

"Then the story of Thomas Marks, the Vam-Wolf-Zom, comes to an abrupt end."

We flew up into the air again and Martha tried to show me how to land.

"Stop flapping your wings, but keep them extended, then glide in, tilting your wings up to reduce speed."

Martha landed perfectly.

My feet hit the floor and I tripped, tumbled over, did five summersaults and banged into the wall.

"Not what I would call a good landing," said Martha. "But a very good crash."

I stood up on my little bat feet. "I suck at this."

"As the wise Dr. Franklin said, 'Energy and persistence conquer all things.' Practice an hour a day and you shall achieve proficiency. And now I cannot delay any longer, I truly must depart."

"Why?"

"I must feed."

"Oh . . . okay. . . . Thanks for the flying lesson."

"You are most welcome. Anything else?"

"Um . . . I don't think so?"

"You do not wish to know how to transform back to human?"

HOW DID I FORGET TO ASK HER THAT?!

"Oh! Yeah! Right! What do I say?"

"'Turn to human. Human, I shall be.'" She flew up to the windowsill. "Farewell and good luck, Thomas Marks. Perhaps our paths will cross again."

"Wait—Martha. One more question."

"*What?*"

"Do you ever wish you . . . weren't a vampire?"

She got serious again. "I did at one time . . . at first. . . . But no longer. I am what I am. Worry not, Thomas. It gets better."

She turned and looked out the window. I think she was checking for owls and hawks. Then, she flew straight out. I watched her soar up over the treetops, past the moon, and off into the night.

I wondered if I was ever going to see her again.

∘ ∘ ∘

I took a deep breath and said, "Turn to human. Human, I will be."

Nothing happened.

I was still a bat.

"Turn to human. Human, I will be."

Why was I still a bat?

"Turn to human. Human, I will be!"

I didn't change!

"TURN TO HUMAN. HUMAN, I WILL BE!"

It wasn't working. I was going to be a bat *forever*.

Emma would put me in a cage! Or sell me to a zoo! I'd have to sleep hanging upside down! I couldn't be in Annie's band! I'd have to be a bat for Halloween for the rest of my life! How was I going to live as a bat?!

"Turn to human! Human, I will be!"

I shouted it.

I whispered it.

I said it fast, slow, backward and forward, over and over.

I was still a tiny little pop-eyed, big-eared, claw-footed bat.

I had a terrible thought. Did Martha go around changing people into vampires, teaching them how to turn into a bat, and then leaving them like that forever? Was Martha Livingston the most evil person in the world?

Maybe I was saying it wrong. What *exactly* did she say? I closed my eyes and pictured her saying it.

"Turn to human. . . . Human, I will— NO! It's not 'will be,' you idiot! It's *shall* be!"

I took a deep breath. "Turn to human. . . . Human, I shall be."

My body felt like it was stretching and all of a sudden I was human again. I double-checked to make sure I didn't still have wings or big ears or bat feet.

I didn't.

I went back upstairs and wrote the wording down on a piece of paper, in case I ever forgot again. Then I got into bed and went to sleep.

I was so glad that I was regular, normal, Vam-Wolf-Zom me.

6.

Showing Zeke

When we drove home, Emma texted her new boyfriend, Carrot Boy, the whole time. He really does look like a carrot. He used to mow our lawn, and Emma made fun of him and gave him the nickname Carrot Boy. Now she's in love with him. She is so bizarre.

I decided not to tell my family or Annie or anybody at school that I could fly until I got better at it. I did want to show Zeke, even though he is not the greatest person in the world at keeping secrets. When I got home, I ran up to my room and called him. He made it to my house in four minutes, which I think is a record. After he came into my room, I locked the door and made him sit on the bed.

I spoke calmly and quietly. "Zeke, do not scream or yell or dance or do jumping jacks when I show you. . . . Okay?"

"Okay, T-Man!" he said, giving a salute. He loves to salute.

I crossed my arms, closed my eyes, and took a breath.

"Turn to bat. Bat, I shall be."

I turned into a bat.

Zeke screamed, yelled, danced, and did jumping jacks all at the same time.

"STOP!" I yelled, looking up at him from the floor. I thought he was going to accidentally stomp on me. He crouched down on the floor, with his chin on the rug.

"You're a bat!" shouted Zeke.

"It is so cool to talk to a bat, T-Man. . . . Wait . . . I mean . . . *Bat-Tom!*"

"Don't call me Bat-Tom."

"But I have to!" said Zeke.

"No, you don't."

"I'd let you call me Bat-Zeke if I was a bat."

"I know you would, but—"

"Let's go outside and you can show me how you fly!"

"No, Martha said I shouldn't."

"Who's Martha?"

"Uh . . . nobody. I haven't flown outside yet. I need to practice more."

I made him sit back on the bed. I flapped my wings, rose up in the air, and flew around the room in a circle. Zeke went crazy again. But I have to admit, if I saw my best friend turn into a bat and fly around his room, I'd get pretty excited too.

"Bat-Tom, this is the greatest thing that has ever happened in the history of the world!"

Zeke is The King of Exaggerators. Emma is The Queen.

He sat back down on the bed and watched me fly around in circles for a while.

"I could watch you do this all night!"

He really would. I crash-landed on the floor and turned back into me. Zeke applauded.

"I'm not very good at landing yet," I said.

"You'll get better, Bat-Tom."

"Zeke, you can't tell *anybody* that I can fly. I want to get good at it, and then I'll show people."

"Okay. Was it hard to learn?"

"Transforming isn't hard, but flying is. Martha showed me—"

"*Who's* Martha?"

"Nobody."

"But you said she showed you."

I couldn't tell Zeke about Martha. I had to make something up.

"Oh, uh, yeah, I was, uh, thinking about a movie called *Martha the . . . Bird Girl.*"

"I've never heard of that. What's it about?"

"Uh. . . . It's . . . It's about a girl named Martha, who's a bird, it's not very good— Hey, do you want to play Rabbit Attack!?"

Zeke's favorite video game in the whole world is Rabbit Attack! It is the most boring video game in the whole world. He knows that I hate to play it. He looked at me, suspicious. Then his eyes got wider and wider.

"Wait. . . . Is Martha the person who taught you how to fly? . . . Is Martha a *vampire*? . . . Is Martha the vampire bat that bit you— She is! She is! She is!"

He started doing jumping jacks again. I let him do them for a while, so he'd wear himself out. I couldn't believe that Zeke figured it out. He surprises me sometimes.

Technically I hadn't told Zeke about Martha. He had guessed on his own, so I hadn't broken the blood oath. That must be why I didn't burst into flames.

I started to tell Zeke about Martha, what she looked like and what we talked about.

"She's two hundred and forty-four years old?!" he said. "Does she look super crusty, wrinkly old?"

"No. She looks about thirteen or fourteen."

"Is Martha gonna be your vampire girlfriend?"

"No!"

Saying "no" never stops Zeke.

"If she *was* your vampire girlfriend, would you marry her when you got older?"

"Zeke, she's *not* going to be my—"

"If you got married, would you have vampire babies? Or would they be two-thirds vampire and one-third werewolf and zombie?"

"I'm not going to marry—"

"Would you name one of your kids Zeke?"

"I'm not going to marry Martha! I'll probably never see her again."

"When'd she become a vampire?"

"In 1776 in Philadelphia. She knew Benjamin Franklin."

Zeke's eyes got huge and his jaw dropped. *"BENJAMIN FRANKLIN WAS A VAMPIRE*?!"

I explained that he wasn't, and Zeke was disappointed, like I knew he would be.

"Aw man," he said. "I wish he was a vampire. History would be so much more interesting."

"I know. So, anyway, Martha loves music. She plays eleven different instruments and—"

"Hey! She can be in our band!"

"Zeke, I *promised* I wouldn't tell anybody about her. So you can't tell *anybody*. Okay?"

He saluted again.

"Okay, Bat-Tom!"

"Don't call me Bat-Tom!"

7.

Band of Five

The next day, just before Zeke and I got on the bus to go to school, I said, "Remember, don't tell anybody I can turn into a bat and fly."

He gave me a thumbs-up, but I wasn't sure he wouldn't.

Some of the kids on the bus gave me weird looks. I'd figured it would take a while until they got used to me being a Vam-Wolf-Zom. I was hoping that eventually some other kid would get abducted by aliens or turn into a robot or get superpowers and nobody would pay any attention to me anymore. Unfortunately, that probably wasn't going to happen.

Zeke and I walked down the aisle toward Annie. She was sitting with Capri Ishibashi, a girl in my Art class who is an amazing artist.

"Hey, guys," said Annie. "Don't forget about band practice next week."

"We won't," I said as we sat down in the seat across from them.

For some reason, when Annie had asked me to sing in her band, she had also asked about half the other kids in our class to be in it too: Abel Sherrill on guitar; Capri on piano; and a tall, skinny kid, with long hair, named Landon, who we used to call Dog Hots, but he told us not to call him that anymore, on drums. Zeke, who didn't play anything, was going to be our roadie.

"Hey, Tom, did you turn into a werewolf on Friday night?" asked Capri.

Annie gave her a dirty look. "Not. Cool. Capri."

"*What*?" said Capri. "There was a full moon. I was just asking."

"It's okay," I said. "Yeah, I turned into a werewolf."

"Can I see you do that sometime?" said Capri. "Or is that a weird thing to ask?"

"*Yes*, Capri," said Annie. "That *is* a weird thing to ask."

"I want to see it too!" said Zeke. "Is it as excellent as when you turn into a—"

I quickly cut Zeke off before he said "bat." "I don't know when the next full moon is."

"It's in three weeks," said Capri. "On Tuesday, October 17, at 6:27 pm."

"You looked that up?" said Annie.

"Maybe," said Capri.

I guess she really wanted to see me turn. I really wanted to change the subject. "What time will practice be, Annie?"

"Four o'clock."

"Our band is going to be so awesome!" said Zeke. I thought he might start doing jumping jacks, so I stepped on his foot so he couldn't.

"Ow!"

"Sorry, Zeke."

o o o

"I don't want any trouble today!" yelled Bus Lady as someone got on the bus.

I knew it was Tanner Gantt. I bet he had a new nickname for me.

"Good morning, Freak Face!"

I was right.

He walked down the aisle toward us, pretending to be afraid.

"Ooo! I better not sit next to Freak Face! He might bite me! Or suck my blood!"

He yanked a little kid out of the seat in front us.

"Hey! I was sitting there!" complained the kid.

"Not anymore," said Tanner Gantt. He sat down, turned around to face us, and hung his big arms over the back of the seat. "How'd it feel to get suspended, Freak Face?"

I ignored him.

Zeke didn't.

"You should know," he said. "You've been suspended a zillion times."

"Shut up, Zimmer-Moron, before I shut you up with my fist." Tanner Gantt turned to me. "So, Freak Face? Eat anybody this weekend?"

"When are you going to grow up, Tanner?" said Annie.

Tanner spun around to face her. "When are *you* gonna . . ."

He tried to think of something clever to say.

". . . gonna . . ."

He couldn't think of anything, so he gave up.

"Is there a problem back there?" said Bus Lady, looking in her rearview mirror.

"No, ma'am!" said Tanner Gantt, using his fake nice voice. "We're just talking about the fun stuff we did this weekend!" He turned back to me. "Did you learn how to turn into a bat and fly yet, Freak Face?"

"No," I lied.

"Ha! I knew you'd be a lame vampire."

I wanted to turn into a bat right there and fly around the bus. Zeke started nudging me with his elbow and whispered, "Do it, do it, do it, do it."

"Hey? What's the name of our band going to be?" asked Capri.

I *really* wished Capri hadn't said anything about our band. I was hoping Tanner Gantt wouldn't find out about it.

"You guys are starting a band?" he said, laughing.

"Yeah. We are," said Annie, proudly. "With Tom and Abel and Dog Hots—I mean Landon."

"I'm the roadie!" said Zeke.

"What's the name of your band?" sneered Tanner Gantt. "The Losers? . . . The Lame-O's? . . . The Dorks? . . . The World's Worst Band? . . . Barstow and the Weirdos? . . . The Band That Sucks? . . . Freak Boy and the Freaks?"

This went on for the whole bus ride to school.

8.

Donuts, Ants, Dogs

Abel Sherrill, the kid who wears a suit and tie to school every day, was at our locker when I got there.

"Good morning, Mr. Marks. I hope your weekend was a restful one after the previous eventful week?"

Abel and Martha Livingston sounded the same. I wanted to tell him about her, but a blood oath is a blood oath.

"It was okay," I said. "I went up to my grandmother's house."

I kept my science and history books, and put

my other books in the locker. Abel had put up a dry-erase board that he wrote stuff on each day. Today it said:

Three can keep a Secret, if two of them are dead.

Benjamin Franklin

"How come you put that up today, Abel?"

"I am a great fan of Benjamin Franklin. A true genius."

Now I *really* wanted to tell him about Martha.

"I hope you don't mind me inquiring," he said as he put a book inside his briefcase, "but have you had any luck with transformation and flying?"

"No. Not yet."

He nodded. "Those must be extremely difficult skills to achieve. How unfortunate you don't have someone skilled in that art to personally instruct you. Well, be seeing you!"

Mr. Prady, my Science teacher, snapped his fingers to get everybody's attention. "Sixth-Grade Science Fair will be in two weeks, for those of you interested in participating. It is not mandatory. You may do it solo or with a partner."

Zeke and I have always done our science fair projects together.

"T-Man! I have the BEST idea for our science project!"

He says that every single year.

We never win.

In first grade we did one called "What Happens When Skittles Dissolve?" You put Skittles in a circle on a plate and then pour hot water in the middle, and you're supposed to see a really cool rainbow. It looked amazing on the Internet. But Zeke ate all the Skittles on the way to school and we had to use his sandwich instead. We changed our project name to "What Happens When a Peanut Butter Sandwich Dissolves?" It was one of the most disgusting things I've ever seen, and we came in thirty-eighth place.

One of the worst ones we did was called "What Music Does My Dog Like Best?" We used my dog, Muffin. We played a bunch of different types of music, but we couldn't tell what he liked best because he just sat there and drooled. Zeke wanted to change the name to "What Music Makes Dogs Drool?" I didn't let him. Then, Muffin ate Maren Nesmith's project, which was right next to ours, called "Which Food Will Mold Fastest?" Muffin ate Maren's rotten banana, a green piece of bread, and some disgusting cheese. We had to take him to the vet to make sure he didn't get sick. We got twenty-seventh place, which was the highest score we ever got. I think we got it because one of the judges thought Muffin was cute.

"What Is the Healthiest Donut?" was another bad idea. Zeke thought we'd win if the judges got to eat donuts. But he left the donuts on his back porch and a million ants showed up. We changed our sign to "Do Ants Like Donuts?" We got thirty-second place. As we stood there, watching the ants crawl all over the donuts, Zeke got an idea for the next science fair. He'd seen a movie about these guys that escaped from a prison, so he wanted to do "Can Ants Escape from an Art Farm?"

I said, "No!"

o o o

"What's your idea this year?" I asked Zeke.

He took a deep breath and tried to make a sound like a drumroll. Except it didn't sound like a drum roll. It sounded like a noisy car. For some reason,

63

Zeke can't do sound effects. When he tries to do a dog bark, it sounds like a chicken. His airplane noise sounds like a trombone, and his bomb noise sounds like a toilet flushing. It doesn't matter to him; he thinks they're all great.

"Zeke, what's your idea?"

He stopped making the noisy car sound. "You!"

"Me?"

"Yes! The World's Only Vam-Wolf-Zom!"

"I don't want to be a science project."

"I would *love* to be a science project!" said Zeke.

"No way!"

"Think about it, T-Man. Nobody else will have anything as cool. We can make charts and you can stand there and I'll point at you with a pointer and say sciency stuff! Then, at the end, you can turn into a bat and fly around the gym! We would totally get first place!"

I wasn't sure I'd be good enough at flying by then.

"Zeke, I'm not going to be a science project."

"Okay," he sighed. "What're we gonna do, then?"

"Nothing stupid or crazy or anything using food or dogs or ants."

9.

The Longest Tale

As soon as I walked into History class, I remembered that I had forgotten to write the *My Favorite American* report. It wasn't my fault. I had been busy learning how to turn into a bat and fly that weekend.

After the tardy bell rang, Mrs. Troller said, "Good morning, ladies and gentlemen. Now, I don't want you to turn in your *My Favorite American* papers today."

I wanted to give her The Greatest Teacher of All Time Award. I let out a big sigh of relief. But then, like every time you think things are going great, she went on.

"What I would like each of you to do instead, is this; read your papers aloud, so everybody gets to hear them."

I immediately took away her Greatest Teacher of All Time Award. Surprise oral reports should be illegal.

"Let's begin," she said.

Teachers usually go in alphabetical order, so I knew Mrs. Troller wouldn't call on me right away. Maybe I could write the report while everybody whose last names started with *A* through *L* were doing theirs. Zeke was so lucky. His last name is Zimmerman, so he always went last.

"Also," said Mrs. Troller, "I dislike going in alphabetical order."

What? I love going in alphabetical order.

"It's not fair," she added.

Yes, it is!

A kid I didn't know raised his hand and said, "I agree, Mrs. Troller, it's not fair at all."

"I thought you'd agree, Mr. Aasen."

Maybe she'd start at the end of the alphabet, and Zeke would have to go first? That would still give me some time.

"Mr. Marks, why don't you start us out?" she said.

I had to go first. I couldn't believe it. I just sat there. I was hoping for a surprise fire drill or earthquake drill or tornado or hurricane or flood or blizzard or snowstorm drill, but nothing happened.

"Mr. Marks?" she said. "Do you have your report?"

I stood up. I grabbed a piece of paper that I had started making a list on, called "Band Names," because I needed something to pretend to read from. Hopefully, Mrs. Troller wouldn't make me hand the paper in.

BAND NAMES

Annie and Tom & The Others

Marks & Barstow

Barstow & Marks

I walked to the front of the room and pretended to read. I decided to speak super slowly, so my report would seem longer.

"My favorite American . . . is . . . Benjamin Franklin. . . . He was a man. . . . He was famous and did a lot of stuff. . . . He made up famous sayings like, 'Three can keep a secret if . . . if you kill two of the people.' . . . And he invented a stove that cooked food, which he called The Ben Franklin Stove. . . . He also invented bifocals, so people could see two things at the same time, and, uh, he proved that lightning had electricity in it when he flew a kite with a key attached to the string."

I looked over at Mrs. Troller and smiled.

"Go on," she said.

I cleared my throat even though I didn't need to. I tried to remember what else Martha had said about Franklin.

"Ben Franklin was a tall man . . . and he lived in Philadelphia. He liked to go to a place called the City Tavern. . . . His favorite waitress was a girl named Martha Livingston. She was thirteen years old and had green eyes and pale skin and long red hair, about the same length that Annie Barstow had before she cut it over the summer."

Why did I say that? I glanced over at Annie, who gave me a weird look.

"Um. . . . One night Ben Franklin left his glasses on the table, and Martha said, 'Oh, no! Ben Franklin left his glasses on the table! I better return them or he won't be able to see clearly and invent more cool stuff!'"

Now Mrs. Troller was giving me weird looks.

"So, she ran after him and she gave him his glasses. He gave her a tip of two pennies and said, 'Thanks, Martha. Now I can go invent more stuff.' And then she headed back to her job and took a shortcut through a dark, scary-looking alley and this man jumped out at her and she screamed."

Some of the kids leaned forward in their seats.

"Ben Franklin heard her scream and so he ran into the alley and saw that she was being attacked by . . ."

Mrs. Troller leaned forward in her chair. ". . . attacked by . . ."

I couldn't say "vampire." What else could she be attacked by? A dog? A robber? A ghost? I looked over at Zeke. He scrunched one of his eyes closed, then he lifted his hand and made a hook with his finger.

"A pirate!" I said. "And Ben Franklin got into a fight with the pirate, who had a hook for a hand . . . and Franklin hit the pirate with his cane. Then, the pirate pulled out his sword. So, Ben Franklin pulled off the top of the cane and it had a sword hidden inside it—he invented that too—and he cut off the pirate's other hand and Martha escaped. . . . And . . . and she lived happily ever after and the pirate got a hook for his other hand and—all the other pirates called him Captain Two Hooks— and the next day Benjamin Franklin signed the Declaration of Independence and America was born, and that's why he is my favorite American. The end."

Zeke clapped.

I walked back to my seat as fast as I could and sat back down.

"That was . . . quite interesting, Mr. Marks," said Mrs. Troller. "Benjamin Franklin is also one of my favorite Americans. I've never heard the story about his fight with the pirate.
Where did you read that?"

"Uh . . . Martha Livingston, the girl . . . she . . . um . . . wrote a diary and I read it."

"I would like to read that diary. Can you bring it in tomorrow?"

"Uh . . . it was online. I'll see if I can find it again."

I could tell that Mrs. Troller didn't believe me. I was going to get an F.

"All right," she said. "Next up let's have Zeke Zimmerman."

Zeke jumped up from his desk and practically

ran to the front of the room. I knew that Zeke's favorite American was either the person who invented Rabbit Attack! or the banjo. He loves banjos. I was betting Mrs. Troller would give him a bad grade too.

For some reason Zeke bowed when he got up there.

"My favorite American is my best friend, Tom Marks, the Vam-Wolf-Zom."

I wanted to turn into a bat and fly out the window. I could have done it. But, I didn't.

Mrs. Troller folded her hands on top of her desk.

"Zeke, the assignment was supposed to be about a person from American history."

"I know, but Tom is an American and he's part of history because he's the only Vam-Wolf-Zom in the world."

Mrs. Troller thought for a second. "I believe you're right. Go on."

Zeke talked about me for ten minutes until Mrs. Troller made him stop. I kept thinking he was going to say I could turn into a bat and fly, but luckily he never did.

Zeke got a B on his report.

I got a C minus.

Life is so totally unfair.

10.

The Masterpiece

Today you will be drawing portraits of each other," said Mr. Baker, my Art teacher.

He showed us some famous portrait paintings. First was the *Mona Lisa*, by a guy named Leonardo da Vinci. Mr. Baker said they keep it in a special sealed box with bulletproof glass. Who would want to shoot a painting? That's crazy.

There was a self-portrait by a woman named Frida Kahlo that was kind of creepy. You could see her heart, inside her body, and a little tube went out to her lap. Some blood was dripping on her dress. The blood made me a little thirsty.

I liked a painting by a guy named Vincent van Gogh. He wore a furry hat and was smoking a pipe and had a white scarf tied around his head. Mr. Baker said Van Gogh was his favorite artist.

"Is Van Gogh the guy who cut his ear off?" asked Elliot Freidman, a kid with thick glasses.

"Ew!" said some kids.

"Actually, he only cut off his ear lobe," said Mr. Baker.

"Why'd he do that?" I asked.

"Van Gogh had serious mental-health challenges. Sometimes he felt angry or sad or depressed and couldn't control himself. He had an argument with his friend, another painter named Paul Gauguin, and attacked him with a razor blade. Then Van Gogh cut off his own ear lobe. Some people think it's because they lived near a bullfighting arena, where matadors cut off bulls' ears. But that is only part of Van Gogh's story. He worked very hard during his short life, producing over two thousand artworks. Unfortunately, he sold only a few paintings when he was alive. Today he is regarded as one of the greatest artists of all time and his art hangs in famous museums around the world. One of his paintings sold for over eighty-two million dollars."

I felt sorry that Van Gogh never knew he got famous. I wish they had real time machines, so I could go back and tell him.

"Mr. Van Gogh?"

"Ja?"

"Do you speak English?"

"Yes. I speak Dutch, French, and English."

"My name's Tom Marks. I came from the future in this Time Machine. I wanted to tell you not to be sad and depressed because no one wants to buy your paintings. You're going to be super famous.

Your paintings will be in museums, millions of people will love your art, and one of your paintings will sell for eighty-two million dollars."

To prove it, I'd take an iPad along and show him pictures of his paintings in museums. I bet he'd be surprised.

"This—this is unbelievable! When will this happen?!"

"In about a hundred thirty years."

"A hundred thirty years?! I will be long dead and gone! I want to be appreciated and rich and famous now! Take me to the future in your Time Machine!"

"Oh. . . . Sorry, I can't. It's a one-seater."

"Now I am even more sad and depressed!"

"Can I buy one of your paintings, Mr. Van Gogh?"

"Yes . . . I guess so."

"How much for the one with the sunflowers?"

"Eighty-two million dollars."

"What?! I don't have eighty-two million dollars. I'm just a kid."

"Well, that's the price! Go back to the future in your stupid Time Machine! Leave me alone!"

Maybe it's better that we don't have real Time Machines.

Then, Mr. Baker said, "As sad as his story is, Van Gogh left us many wonderful works of art. So, let's honor his memory by making our own works of art."

Everybody wanted Capri to do their portrait, because she's the best artist in the class, but she said she wanted to draw me. I guess I was lucky for once. Nobody wanted me to draw their portrait because they all know I'm the worst artist in the class. I ended up drawing Elliot. I did it fast, because I wanted Capri to have plenty of time to draw me. He didn't like it.

"That doesn't look like me! It looks like my dad!"

"Well, give it to your dad for his birthday or Father's Day."

Since I'm one-third vampire, I can't see myself in a mirror. It's just blurry. Vampires don't cast a reflection for some reason. And you can't take a picture of a vampire either. I should have asked Martha why.

Anyway, I had no idea what I looked like since I became a Vam-Wolf-Zom, but now I would.

Capri started sketching me with her pencil.

"Make it super realistic," I said.

"Okay," said Capri.

"I want to know *exactly* what my face looks like."

"Got it."

"And use some colored pencils, so I can see what my skin looks like."

"I will!"

"And show my fangs and get my ears right."

For no reason, she started yelling at me. "Stop talking and hold still! I can't draw you if you're going to talk the whole time!"

Capri is a very temperamental artist.

I sat there and started to think. *Was this a good idea? Did I really want to know what I looked like? What if I looked as horrible and disgusting as Emma said I did?*

Mom and Dad said I didn't look bad, but parents have to say their kids look good. Zeke said I looked awesome, but he's my best friend, and, well . . . he's Zeke. He thinks Randee Rabbit, a character in the video game Rabbit Attack!, looks awesome. Trust me, he doesn't.

"Done," said Capri.

I was a little afraid to look. She handed me the picture and I took a deep breath. I was going to see what I looked like for the very first time.

o o o

I definitely looked like a Vam-Wolf-Zom.

I didn't look as bad as I thought I would, but I didn't look better either.

"Capri, are my fangs really that big?"

"Yeah. But you only see them when you smile."

"And my skin is that color?"

"Well, I didn't have the exact shade of gray-green pencil I needed."

I looked closer. "Is my hair that thick and does it stick up all over the place?"

"Yeah. But you could comb it."

She had a point. I could do that.

"Are my eyes watery?"

"A little. But you only notice it if you get really close."

"And my ears are that pointy?"

"I like your ears." Her face went red for some reason.

I started to think that maybe I should get braces. And contact lenses. Or wear a wig.

Mr. Baker walked by. "Nicely done, Capri. You *really* captured Tom's face."

"Thanks, Mr. Baker. Do we have to hand these in or can we take them home?"

"You may take them home."

Carpi held the drawing out to me. "Do you want to have this?"

I wasn't sure I wanted it. But maybe Capri would get famous someday, like Van Gogh. It might be worth a lot of money.

"Sure," I said. "Thanks. Make sure you sign it."

She signed her name at the bottom.

I looked at the drawing again. This is what I was going to look like for the rest of my life. Maybe it was better I couldn't see myself in mirrors or photographs.

o o o

At lunch, I showed Capri's drawing to Zeke and Abel, at our usual table in the cafeteria.

"Tell me the truth, guys," I said. "Is that what I really look like?"

Zeke looked at it. "Uh . . . well . . . um . . . sorta . . . kinda . . . in a way . . . maybe. . . . Yeah!"

Abel stroked his chin and said, "There is no question whatsoever, Mr. Marks, it is unmistakably

you. However, one must remember, this is Capri's artistic interpretation of your visage. How she sees you in her mind's eye."

I'm not sure what he meant, but he's smart, so he probably was right.

11.

Tea Party

In Phys Ed I ran the track wearing my hat, sunglasses, and sunscreen. I could have run faster than everybody, but I didn't try. What was the point? And I didn't want to be a showoff.

Zeke and I were running next to each other when Tanner Gantt ran up and said, "Hey, Three Freak!"

I bet he had spent all of lunch thinking up that name.

He laughed. "Get it? You're a *Three* Freak!"

"Yeah," I said.

"You're Three Freak because you're *three* things."

"I get it! You don't have to explain it!"

"Cut the chitchat, Marks!" yelled Coach Tinoco, from across the field. "You're supposed to be running! Not having a tea party!"

Why did Coach say we were having a tea party? We weren't pretending to be drinking tea. I've never been to a tea party. I don't even like tea.

Tanner Gantt went on. "You're Three Freak *because* you're a vampire, a werewolf, and a zombie."

"I know what I am, you _____!"

And then I said a word that you're not allowed to say at school. Or at my house. Dad gets to say it. Gram says it sometimes. Emma's said it to me, but she's always careful that Mom and Dad don't hear her.

"Coach!" yelled Tanner Gantt. "Did you hear what Tom Marks just called me?!"

"I did! Three more laps, Marks!" yelled Coach.

"See ya later, Three Freak," said Tanner Gantt as he ran ahead.

I ran the three laps superfast. I didn't care if anybody thought I was a showoff.

 o o o

On the way to Choir, I showed Capri's drawing of me to Annie.

"Wow," she said. "She is an awesome artist. She should do the posters for our band."

"Is that what I really look like?" I asked.

Annie looked at me and then back at the drawing. "Not *exactly*. . . . But I'd know it was you."

I didn't know whether that was good news or bad news.

Annie handed me the drawing. "So, how come Capri gave it to you?"

I shrugged. "I don't know. But I'm gonna keep it. Maybe she'll get famous like that Van Gogh guy."

"He's my favorite artist," said Annie.

"Really?" I said. "Did you know he did two thousand artworks, but only sold a few paintings his whole life?"

"I know. It's so sad. And he cut off his ear."

"Actually it was just his ear lobe."

"Really? I didn't know that."

We talked about Van Gogh all the way to Choir. Sometimes school actually teaches you stuff that you can use in life.

○ ○ ○

In Choir we practiced singing "What a Wonderful World." Mr. Stockdale rolled over to his desk in his wheelchair to play it for us on the computer. He was in a surfing accident when he was twenty-five and his legs were paralyzed. He can't walk anymore, but he still goes surfing and paddle boarding.

"The man who sings this song is named Louis

Armstrong," said Mr. Stockdale. "Has anyone ever heard of him?"

Nobody raised a hand. I had accidentally howled on the first day of choir and Mr. Stockdale got mad at me, so I wanted to get on his good side. I raised my hand.

"Yes, Mr. Marks?"

"Louis Armstrong was a famous musician who sang and played the trumpet. He was one of the greatest jazz artists of all time. He played on riverboats on the Mississippi River in New Orleans."

Mr. Stockdale looked surprised. "That is true."

"He did another song called 'Mr. Potato Head Blues.'"

Mr. Stockdale smiled. "I believe the correct title is '*Potato* Head Blues.' I'm very impressed, Mr. Marks."

I glanced over at Annie. She looked like she was impressed too.

"How did you know that?" he asked.

"This girl I met told me. She saw him play once on a riverboat."

"A *girl*?" said Mr. Stockdale, who look confused. "How old was she?"

I almost said she was two hundred and forty-four, but luckily I didn't. "She's thirteen."

"Well, she couldn't have seen Louis Armstrong play in person. He died in 1971. Unless she has a Time Machine."

Some kids laughed.

"Oh. . . . Yeah. . . . Right. I meant she saw a video of him on YouTube."

The bell rang and I was glad to hear it.

Then I went home and The Most Disgusting, Grossest, Make You Want to Throw Up Thing happened.

12.

Art Critics

When I got home from school, I dropped my stuff on the kitchen table. Capri's drawing of me was sticking up from the top of my backpack, and Emma yanked it out. She's always grabbing my stuff.

"What is this?" she demanded.

"Nothing, Grabby Magee," I said. I didn't try to grab it back because I didn't want it to get ripped or torn in half, in case it was going to be worth $82,500,000 someday.

"Did you *really* do this?" she said, looking at it.

I could tell she was jealous. Emma can't draw either, but she thinks she can. At least I know I can't draw. Last summer she did these ugly paintings of flowers. Mom said we had to tell her they were good, so we wouldn't hurt her feelings. I told Mom that Emma has no feelings.

Emma looked up at me. "Did your Vam-Wolf-Zom powers make you a good artist?"

"Maybe they did." Technically, I wasn't lying. I just wanted to see Emma get mad.

"That is so unfair!" she said, and tossed the drawing on the table.

Mom came in and saw the drawing and acted like I was The World's Greatest Artist. "Tom, this is wonderful. I had no idea you could draw like this. We have a *real* artist in the family."

Emma glared at Mom. "Hey! What about *me*?"

"Oh. well, yes, of course, you too, Emma. Your flower paintings were very . . . special."

Mom is the worst liar in the world.

"Hey, wait a minute," said Emma. "How'd you see yourself to draw this? You can't see your reflection in mirror."

"Okay, I didn't draw it," I confessed.

"I knew it!" said Emma. She was lying. She thought I'd done it. Doesn't she ever get tired of lying?

"This girl named Capri did it," I said.

"Is she your *girlfriend*?" said Emma.

I knew she was going to say that.

"No!"

"Then why'd she put a little heart over the 'i'?"

I hadn't noticed that. Did Capri always do that?

"That's just the way she writes her name," I lied.

"Why didn't you ask *me* to draw your portrait?" said Emma.

Mom and I looked at each other.

"Well . . ." said Mom, "maybe you can do a portrait of Tom too. I'm sure he'd love that."

No, I wouldn't. Mom was crazy. Emma would make me look worse than I already do. Mom took Capri's picture and stuck it up on the refrigerator with some magnets that looked like sushi. Emma freaked out.

"Seriously? I have to look at Tom's face every day, I don't need a picture of him too. And in the kitchen? This is where we eat!"

"You don't have to look at it, Emma," said Mom.

Emma grumbled. Then she said, "Hey? Why didn't you ever put up any of my flower paintings?"

⚬ ⚬ ⚬

Later that night, I was up in my room when Mom walked by with a box under her arm.

"Mom, when's dinner? I'm starving!"

"Your dad's picking up pizza. He'll be here any minute. Hey, do you want to wear this for Halloween? It's brand-new."

She held up the box. Inside was a Creepy Clown mask and costume. She finds stuff at yard sales and thrift stores, and sells it on eBay.

"Uh, maybe. I haven't decided what I'm going to be yet. You told Dad no garlic, right?"

"Tom, he knows you're part vampire and allergic

to garlic. Hey, will you please clean Terrence's cage?"

"He's not my mouse. He's Emma's."

"I *know* whose mouse he is, Tom."

"Then why do I have to clean his cage?"

"Because I can smell it from here and it smells like it needs to be cleaned."

○ ○ ○

Emma has a mouse named Terrence. She named him after that *stupid* actor in that *stupid* movie that every *stupid* teenage girl saw a million times last year. It was about these two kids in high school who hated each other at first, and then fell in love. Just like Emma and Carrot Boy. Well, actually Emma didn't hate Carrot Boy, but she thought he was super-weird looking.

It was The Worst Movie Ever Made. The only reason I went was because Emma wanted to see it for the hundredth time, and my parents wouldn't let her go alone. She paid me five dollars to go see it with her. After we saw it she told me that was my birthday present, even though my birthday was seven months away. Seeing that movie was the last thing I would have wanted for my birthday.

Emma is The Worst Gift Giver.

The actor that Emma loved was named Terrence, so that's why she named her mouse that.

The only reason Emma had a mouse was because this girl named Claire Devi had one. Emma thinks Claire is The Queen of Everything and she has to do whatever Claire does.

Claire was at our house, the day after we saw The Worst Movie Ever Made, and said, "Oh my God, Emma, you've GOT to get a mouse! They are SO cute! You can put them on your desk when you study! And watch TV with them in your lap!"

Emma bought a mouse that night.

∘ ∘ ∘

Emma paid attention to Terrence the Mouse for about three days and then she was over him. She is The Worst Pet Owner Ever. Mom and Dad have to remind Emma to feed him and give him water and clean his cage because it's filled with poop and pee.

"Where's Emma?" I said to Mom. "Why can't she clean it like she's supposed to?"

"She's at her violin lesson."

"She sucks at the violin."

"Please don't say 'suck.'"

"Okay, she is The Worst Violin Player in the World. *Why* is she still taking lessons?"

"So she'll get better."

"Mom, she'll *never* get better. She never practices. She could take lessons for a million years and she'd still be the worst violinist of all time."

Mom let out a sigh. "Tom, just clean Terrence's cage."

I let out a bigger sigh. "Okay . . ."

"Thank you."

The only reason Emma was taking violin lessons was because she saw *another stupid movie* on TV about this woman who played the violin and all these men fell in love with her. Emma bases her whole life on movies and TV shows. I am not exaggerating.

So, I went to clean Terrence's cage and this gross thing happened, but I can't be completely blamed.

Five Reasons It Wasn't My Fault

1. *Mom and Dad hadn't made dinner.*
2. *Emma hadn't cleaned Terrence's cage like she was supposed to.*
3. *Mom hadn't let me eat anything before dinner, which should be against the law if your son is one-third zombie.*
4. *Dad was late bringing home the pizza.*
5. *Claire Devi told Emma to get a mouse.*

I knew that the reason Dad was late with the pizza was because he went to a store called The

Sound Experience. It's right across the street from Pizza Paul's. It sells vinyl records by bands that no one has ever heard of, except old people, like Dad and Gram and maybe Martha Livingston. So, while Dad was having a great time looking at old records, his part-zombie son was at home, *starving to death*.

So, there I was, upstairs in Emma's room, cleaning Terrence's cage. She hadn't cleaned the cage in a million years. The sawdust was filled with disgusting poop and pee. I felt sorry that Terrence had to live in these conditions.

"Hey, Terrence," I said. "I'm cleaning your cage *again* because Emma never does. If it wasn't for me and my mom, you'd probably starve to death. Or die of exposure to your own toxic waste." I thought about reporting Emma to somebody so they would give her a fine or maybe even put her in jail, but I wasn't sure who to call.

I took Terrence out of the cage and put him in a shoebox with some new shoes Emma had just bought. I secretly hoped he would poop or pee on her shoes. I dumped out the dirty sawdust into the trash can and put in new, fresh sawdust. I love the way new sawdust smells. That's the only enjoyable part of cleaning his cage. Then, I sniffed something that smelled even better.

Terrence.

o o o

I looked down at Terrence, sitting in Emma's shoebox. He's a chubby, little white mouse, with brown eyes and a pink tail. He looked pretty cute. He also looked pretty tasty.

Remember: I didn't ask to be bitten by a zombie. Or a vampire. Or a werewolf.

And don't forget that Emma is The Laziest Person in the World and does not take care of her pet.

If she ever finds anyone to marry her, which I doubt will happen, unless Carrot Boy marries her—and I would seriously think about warning him not to—but if she does get married and have kids, they are going to have to learn to fend for themselves. After a week or two she'll forget to feed them or bathe them or put clothes on them or she'll just get bored with them. I'll probably have to help raise them.

She'll say, "Sorry, kids, I can't feed you today, I'm going out. I'll call up Uncle Tommy and he'll bring some pizza over. But remember it won't have any garlic, because he's a disgusting Vam-Wolf-Zom."

Thinking about pizza made me really hungry.

And then it happened.

I couldn't help it.

I ate Terrence.

13.

Eating Terrence

It took like two seconds. I opened my mouth, tossed him in, and swallowed him whole. I have to admit, Terrence was delicious. But as soon as I ate him, I regretted it. I had to do something so nobody would ever find out. Especially Emma. So, I tried to come up with a plan.

No One Can Find Out I Ate Terrence Plan

I had just come up with the name of the plan when I heard the front door open. It was Emma.

"Dinner better be ready, because I am starving!" she yelled.

"How about you try that again?" said Mom, in a calm voice from the kitchen.

"Good evening, my dear, sweet, lovely mother," said Emma. "What delicious dinner have you prepared for your grateful daughter who adores you?"

"Dad's getting pizza," said Mom.

"I don't want pizza. I'm in the mood for sushi."

"Well, get in the mood for pizza."

I went halfway down the stairs to listen to Mom and Emma in the kitchen.

"How was violin practice, Emma?"

"I'm quitting violin."

"What? Why?"

"It's too hard!"

Emma quits EVERYTHING.

So far, she has *quit* the following:

Ballet (She said the shoes hurt.)
Gymnastics (She said the gym smelled.)
Piano (She said the piano teacher smelled.)

Ribbon dancing (She said it was boring. I could have told her that.)

Harp (She said it was too hard.)

Karate (She didn't like the way she looked in her gi.)

Irish step dancing (She got tired after five minutes.)

The front door opened and Dad *finally* walked in with dinner. He had a pizza box in one hand and a yellow bag from The Sound Experience in the other.

"Pizza! Pizza! Pizza!" he yelled.

I wasn't starving anymore, since I had just eaten The Mouse Who Shall Not Be Named, but I had to pretend to be hungry.

"Dad, what took you so long?" I said as I followed him into the kitchen.

"Let's eat!" said Dad, ignoring my question.

Emma grabbed the pizza box from him like she always does.

Dad held up the Sound Experience bag. "I got a

rare Bob Dylan album for Gram's birthday. We can give it to her when we go up for Thanksgiving."

I *almost* said, "I know a girl who saw Dylan's first concert in New York." Luckily, I didn't.

"Emma," said Mom, "thank your brother for cleaning Terrence's cage."

"I was going to clean it as soon as I got home," said Emma.

There is *no way* Emma would have cleaned his cage. Normally I would have said, "I clean his cage all the time! Even though he's *not* my pet!" But I didn't want to talk about Terrence.

"Hey, how is Terrence?" asked Dad.

No one had asked about Terrence for months.

"He is such a cutie," said Mom. "Emma, remember how you used to put him on your lap and watch TV?"

Emma had only done that once, the first night she got him. Terrence peed on her. She got *really* mad because she was wearing a brand-new pair of jeans (that Clare Devi had told her she HAD to buy). It was pretty funny. She never put him on her lap again.

"How old is Terrence?" asked Dad.

"Good question," said Mom. "How long have you had him, Emma?"

Emma shrugged. "I don't know."

Why was everyone so interested in Terrence? But they had given me an idea.

"He's *really* old," I said. "I was looking at his face. He's got a lot of wrinkles."

"Mice don't get wrinkles," said Emma, who was suddenly a mouse expert.

I ignored her. "He's had a long, happy life. I bet he's going to get some disease soon. I hope he doesn't go on forever, suffering. I hope he just goes quickly. You know, he could be suffering right now and we don't even know it."

"Oh my God, that is *so* morbid," said Emma.

Muffin trotted in and stared at me. He started sniffing. I think he could smell Terrence, even though he was inside my stomach.

I needed to launch the plan.

14.

The Terrence Plan

My plan was perfect. Nobody would know I ate Terrence. But first, I had to get Emma to go upstairs and look in Terrence's cage. She probably hadn't looked in there for months.

"Go up and look at Terrence's face, right now, Emma," I said. "He's old. He has wrinkles."

"He does not."

"I bet you five dollars he does."

She ran upstairs.

"I don't like you two betting," said Mom.

"They have to start someday," said Dad.

"Mom! Dad!" yelled Emma from upstairs. "Tom left Terrence's cage open and he got out!"

Dad stood up and said, "The game is afoot! The Mysterious Case of the Missing Mouse has begun!"

"Don't worry, Emma, we won't give up until we find him!" said Mom.

o o o

We looked for about fifteen minutes and then we gave up. Of course, nobody found Terrence because he was in my stomach. We all sat back down around the kitchen table. It felt like we were four detectives who couldn't solve a case because one of us had done it.

Me.

Mom patted Emma's hand. "He'll turn up, Emma."

No, he wouldn't.

"Do you think Muffin could've eaten him?" asked Dad.

Everybody looked at Muffin. Maybe I could blame him? He did have a guilty look on his face.

"I bet he did!" I said.

"No," said Mom. "Terrence has gotten out before and Muffin just stares at him. He wouldn't eat him."

Thanks a lot, Mom.

Then Emma gave me a strange look. "Wait a minute. . . . Did *you* eat Terrence?"

"What?" I said, as innocently as I could. "Are you crazy?"

"Emma!" said Mom.

"Did you?!" said Emma.

"No, I didn't eat Terrence! Gross! That's disgusting! Eat a mouse? Yuck!"

I was pretty good at lying. I learned from Emma.

"You big fat liar!" she said.

Apparently, she didn't think I was good at lying.

"Zombies eat anything!" she said. "And were-wolves eat animals! And vampires maybe. I don't know, maybe they do!"

"Everybody calm down," said Mom. "Tom would not eat Terrence."

Emma seemed to believe her. Then, she looked like she was going to cry. She's good at fake crying. I could see her trying to win an Academy Award for Best Crying for a Lost Pet Mouse That She Didn't Really Care About.

She let out a sigh that sounded real. She did look sad. I started to feel guilty. Maybe she liked Terrence? Maybe, when she was alone in her room, she talked to him?

"Terrence, I want to tell you a deep, dark secret. You know how I'm not a very nice person? How I lie all the time, complain, exaggerate, and make fun of Tom and I'm mean to him. . . . Well . . . it's because I'm not a human being, I'm from another planet!"

That probably didn't happen, but I still felt bad.

"Sorry, Emma," I said. "I thought I closed the cage door. . . . Maybe Terrence was sick and knew he was going to die, so he went off somewhere to be alone? I bet that's what happened. I think I read somewhere about mice doing that."

Dad looked at me with an "I don't think mice do that" expression.

Emma said, "Maybe he ran away so he could be free and go live in the wild."

Why didn't I think of that? That was a much better reason than going off to die.

"Or maybe Tom's right and he went off to die," she said.

Of course, where he went off to die was my stomach, but I wasn't going to tell her that.

"I guess I probably could've taken better care of him," she added. Emma never admits she is wrong about anything.

I felt like I had to say something. "I'll buy you a new mouse if you want."

"No, thanks," said Emma. "I don't want another mouse. To be honest, Terrence *was* kind of boring. I mean, he didn't really do anything."

What had she expected Terrence to do? Be like the mice in *Cinderella* and sing songs and sew her a dress for the big dance?

"And he did pee on me that time," she said.

I left the three of them at the table and went upstairs to the bathroom to brush my teeth. I only felt about fifty percent better about swallowing

Terrence. But, then the grossest, most disgusting thing ever happened.

I burped.

Then I started to cough.

And then . . .

I threw up Terrence.

15.

Terrence Lives!

Terrence was still alive. I caught him in my hand. He looked up at me like he was really mad. I quickly rinsed him off in the sink and ran downstairs to the kitchen, where Mom and Emma were sitting. Dad was coming in the back door, after going to look in the backyard.

"Look!" I yelled. "I found Terrence!"

"The case is solved!" said Dad.

Mom jumped up out of her chair. "Oh, Terrence! I am so glad to see you!"

"Where'd you find him?" asked Emma, who

stayed in her chair and didn't look that happy to see him.

"In the bathroom," I said. "He was in the cupboard under the sink."

"I looked there," said Dad.

"Well, uh, he must be really good at hiding," I said, and handed Terrence to Emma.

"Ew!" she said. "Why is he wet?"

"I don't know. Maybe there's a leak in the sink?"

Emma held him up to her face. "He doesn't have wrinkles. You owe me five bucks."

I hadn't thought of our bet.

Then, Terrence pooped in Emma's hand.

She screamed and dropped him on the floor. I swear that Terrence gave me a dirty look. He ran in between Dad's feet and raced out the open back door as fast as he could. With my night vision I saw him run across the backyard and under the fence to freedom.

Terrence the Mouse was gone.

Dad solemnly turned to us and said, "Terrence . . . has left the building."

○ ○ ○

That night, I looked up "Can you swallow a mouse?" on the Internet. I found out there used to be a real guy named The Great Waldo, from Germany, who performed in sideshows and circuses and carnivals. He swallowed fish, frogs, mice, and rats, and then regurgitated them back up again. It sounded like a disgusting job, but I guess The Great Waldo didn't mind. Maybe he just wanted to be famous and that was the only thing he could think of.

I wondered about Terrence. What was he thinking when he ran out of our house?

I'm free! Free at last! I have escaped from that house of evil! Kept in a cage! Wallowing in my own filth! Ignored! Eaten by a savage beast! But I shall have the last laugh. . . . I have a plan. . . . I'll go to that old scientist across the street, the Professor Beiersdorfer they talk about. I will find a concoction or machine that will make me into a giant fifty-foot-tall monster mouse! It may take weeks, months, years! I don't care! Be afraid, Tom and Emma, be very afraid. . . . For one dark night, I shall return and have my vengeance. I will put you in a cage, Emma! You shall wallow in your own poop! And as for you, Tom, I shall eat you as you ate me! Let's see how you like that! Revenge is sweet! Ha! Ha! Ha! Ha!

I hoped Terrence didn't do that.

16.

Zeke Almost Has a Heart Attack

I kept practicing flying and landing in my room at night over the next week.

On Thursday, after school, Zeke and I were walking to my house from the bus stop. Our first band practice was in half an hour at Annie's house. I didn't tell Zeke about eating Terrence. It was pretty embarrassing, not to mention gross.

"Do you think our band's gonna be famous, Bat-Tom?"

"Zeke, please don't call me that."

"Sorry. I've tried, but I just can't help it."

"We might get famous," I said. "Annie's a great singer and guitarist. She said Abel's a really good guitar player, and Dog Hots is good on drums, and I think Capri takes classical piano lessons."

We got to my house and my mom was unloading a box from her van into the garage, where she stores the stuff she sells on eBay.

"Hi, Mrs. Marks," said Zeke. "Do you need some help?"

"Thank you, Zeke, this is the last box. Hey, Tom, did you notice anything new on the bumper of the van?"

There was a bumper sticker that said:

Mom smiled. "Dad has one too."

"Uh . . . thanks, Mom."

It was sort of nice and embarrassing at the same time.

"I wanna get one too!" said Zeke.

I reminded him that I wasn't his son and he didn't have a car.

"Oh, yeah. Right," he said. "Wait! I know! I'll get one that's says, 'Proud *Friend* of a Vam-Wolf-Zom' and put it on my skateboard."

"I thought it got stolen? Did you get it back?"

"No. But if I ever get it back, I'll put that on it."

Mom reached into the back of the van. "Zeke, I found something today that you might be interested in." She pulled out a long, leather black bag.

"Excellent! A big, black bag! Thanks, Mrs. M, I can totally use that."

It doesn't take much to get Zeke excited.

She smiled and then unzipped the bag and pulled out an old, beat-up banjo.

Zeke almost had a heart attack. His eyes got big; his mouth opened wider than I thought was possible; he started shaking and hyperventilating, that thing when you breathe really fast. I thought I might have to call 911.

"A BANJO!" he screamed, and started jumping up and down. He jumped higher than I'd ever seen him go before. Maybe he should try out for basketball?

He stopped jumping. "Can I . . . can I touch it?"

"Of course," she said.

Zeke slowly reached out and touched it with the tips of his fingers.

"It feels . . . banjo-y."

I don't think "banjo-y" is a real word.

"How much are you going to sell it for on eBay, Mrs. Marks?" he asked.

Mom winked at me.

"I'm not going to sell it, Zeke. I'm going to give it to you."

Zeke looked like he was going to faint.

"Really, Mrs. Marks? Seriously? Honestly?"

"It's yours, Zeke. Let's call it an early birthday gift."

Zeke started crying. I knew he was crying because he was happy, but I was sort of embarrassed for him. I don't like to see people cry. Especially when it's a friend, or your parents or any old person, or even Emma (though she's usually faking it). There are only five times when it's okay to cry. I made a list.

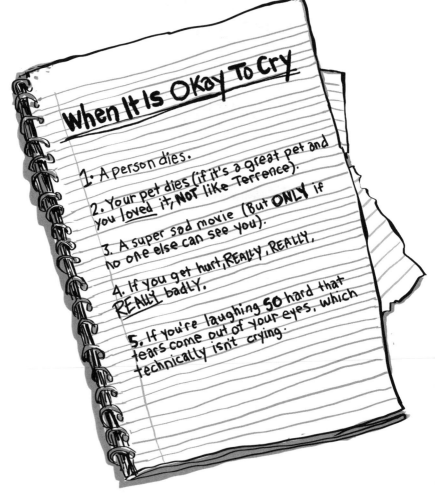

When It Is Okay To Cry

1. A person dies.

2. Your pet dies (if it's a great pet and you loved it, NOT like Terrence).

3. A super sad movie (But ONLY if no one else can see you).

4. If you get hurt, REALLY, REALLY, REALLY badly.

5. If you're laughing SO hard that tears come out of your eyes, which technically isn't crying.

Zeke wasn't embarrassed about crying in front of people. He never gets embarrassed about anything. Sometimes I wish I was more like Zeke, but not the banjo, Rabbit Attack!, jumping jacks part. He wiped his eyes with his shirtsleeve. He was looking at the banjo like it was made of solid gold.

He gave her a hug. "Thanks, Mrs. Marks. . . . This is the best gift I ever got."

"You're very welcome, Zeke."

"C'mon, Zeke," I said. "We gotta go to Annie's. You can leave the banjo here."

"No way! I'm gonna bring it!"

"Why? You don't know how to play it yet."

"You never know when you might need a banjo!"

17.

The Band

Zeke and I were the first ones to get to Annie's house.

"I didn't know you played banjo, Zeke," Annie said when she opened the door.

"I don't!" he said with a big smile, holding up his banjo. "I'm going to learn."

I couldn't see Zeke sitting still long enough to learn how to play the banjo. The only thing he does that for is when he plays Rabbit Attack!

Abel showed up with his guitar and a big, giant amplifier. He still had his suit and tie on. Did he

ever wear regular clothes? I started to pick up the amplifier to take it inside, but Zeke stopped me.

"Hey! I'm supposed to be the roadie!"

I let him carry it in and it took him forever, huffing and puffing and getting red in the face. We set everything up in Annie's living room. There was a piano there for Capri, who hadn't arrived yet. On top of the piano was a picture of Annie from last year, when she had long hair and no glasses. I was looking at it when she came up to me.

"Tom, I only have one microphone. We'll have to share it, is that okay?"

"Sure. I don't mind."

Annie tuned her guitar and Abel noticed Zeke's banjo on the sofa.

"And who amongst you plays the banjo?" he asked.

"Nobody!" said Zeke cheerfully. "But I'm gonna learn."

"Marvelous instrument. Originated in the Caribbean, via West Africa, in the seventeenth century. I play a bit of banjo. May I, Mr. Zimmerman?"

"Sure!" Zeke handed it to him. Abel tuned it and started playing. He was pretty good.

"How many instruments do you play?" I asked.

"I haven't taken a tally, to be perfectly honest. Perhaps six?"

"Tom knows a girl who can play eleven instruments!" said Zeke.

I gave him a dirty look. He didn't see it. He never does.

"What girl?" said Annie.

"This girl that Tom met up at his grandmother's house," said Zeke.

"Is she the same girl who told you about that jazz guy, Louis Armstrong?" asked Annie.

"Yeah," I answered. "So, what song should we do first?"

Annie tuned her guitar again, even though she'd already tuned it. "What's her name?"

"I forget."

"It's Martha Livingston," said Zeke. "And she's—"

I had to make sure Zeke didn't say "She's the vampire bat girl that bit Tom!"

"She's just this girl," I said.

"How old is she?" asked Annie.

"Thirteen."

"What does she look like?"

Why was Annie asking me all these questions?

"I don't remember," I said.

"I do!" said Zeke. "You said she has super-green eyes and red hair, and it's really long like Annie used to have before she cut it. And guess what else?"

I was ready to kill Zeke.

That's when Dog Hots arrived. I'd never been so happy to see him in my life.

"Hey, look!" I shouted. "Dog Hots is here!"

"Don't call me Dog Hots anymore," he said. "Call me Landon."

"Sorry. It's hard to remember. We've been calling you Dog Hots since third grade."

He was carrying a snare drum and a pair of drumsticks.

"Do you want us to help you bring the rest of your drums in?" asked Annie.

Zeke jumped up. "I'm the roadie! I'll get 'em!"

"No. This is it," said Landon.

"What do you mean?" said Annie. "Where are the rest of your drums?"

He held up the snare drum and the drumsticks. "This is all I have."

"I thought you had a drum set with cymbals and everything. You only have one snare drum?"

Dog Hots—I mean Landon—nodded. "Yeah."

"We're not a marching band!" said Annie.

"I love marching bands!" said Zeke. He really did.

Annie was getting upset. "Why didn't you tell me you didn't have a drum set?"

"You didn't ask me," said Landon. "I was just tapping a beat on my desk and you said, 'You play drums?' And I said, 'Yeah.'"

"Drums! With an 's'! Plural! Not singular!" said Annie. "I said 'Can you play *drums!*' Not 'Can you play a drum?'"

Landon shrugged. "Well, sorry. That's all I have."

I didn't care that Landon only had one drum. I was just glad we weren't talking about Martha Livingston anymore.

Annie was getting angry. "What band has a drummer with only one drum?!"

"Our band!" said Zeke. He is always optimistic. Even when it doesn't make any sense.

"You need a drum set, Dog Hots!" yelled Annie.

"My name is *Landon!*"

"Okay! You need a drum set, *Landon!*"

"I don't have one, *Annie!*"

"I know!" shouted Zeke. "We can make a drum set out of trash cans!"

"I'm not playing trash cans!" said Landon.

Everybody was yelling when the front door opened and Capri came in.

"Sorry I'm late— Whoa, what's going on?"

"Landon only has *one* drum!" said Annie.

"Are you kidding me?" said Capri.

"It's not my fault. Drum sets are expensive," said Landon.

"Perhaps you could ask for a drum set for your birthday?" suggested Abel.

"When is it, Landon?" asked Annie.

"March thirteenth."

"That's too far away!"

"Put drum set on your Christmas list," I said.

"That's three months away!" said Annie.

Zeke started bouncing up on and down on the sofa. "I got an idea! Tom's dad has an old drum set in their attic. Maybe you can use it."

"I'll ask my dad," I said.

Everybody calmed down a little.

Annie's mom came in, holding a tray. "Who's hungry? I made quesadillas."

"¡Que maravilloso!" said Abel. "Me encantan las quesadillas."

Annie's mom smiled. "¿Hablas español?"

"Si, Señora Barstow."

I didn't know Abel spoke Spanish. I guess I shouldn't be surprised. I ate three quesadillas. Annie's mom didn't say anything about me being a Vam-Wolf-Zom, which I appreciated.

"Okay. This is important," said Zeke, with a mouthful of quesadilla. "What's our name going to be?"

"It's gotta be . . . *awesome!*" said Capri.

"Yeah, it does," said Annie. "Wait. Do you mean that our band name is the word Awesome? Or do you mean our name's gotta be awesome, like an amazing name?"

"The second one," said Capri. "But Awesome is a cool name. I vote for Awesome."

I shook my head. "We can't use that. People would say, 'You guys better be awesome if you call yourself Awesome.' And it makes us sound stuck-up."

"And Tanner Gantt would make fun of us," said Annie.

"He'll make fun of us no matter what we call ourselves," I pointed out.

"Let's call ourselves Tanner Gantt!" said Zeke. "Then he can't make fun of us."

"NO!" said everybody (except Zeke).

"Let's just shout out names and see what we come up with," said Annie.

Everyone started shouting out different names.

"The Five of Us."

"The Music People."

"That is the *worst* name!"

"The Boogers."

"No! That's gross."

"The Band That Only Has One Drum."

"The Quesadillas."

"No!"

"The Electric Quesadillas?"

"Stop saying quesadilla, Zeke!"

"Annie and the Others."

"Beiersdorfer."

Capri laughed. "What is a Buy-urs-dorfer?"

"He's this scary scientist guy who lives across from Tom who wanted to turn us into robots," said Zeke.

"No, he didn't, Zeke," I said. "My sister made that up."

"How is Emma?" said Landon. "She's cool."

"No, she isn't," I said.

"Let's call ourselves How Is Emma?"

"No!"

"Skeleton Nightmare?"

"What about The Rabbit Attackers? Or The Jumping Jacks? Or The Banjo People?"

(Guess who suggested those ideas?)

"Two Girls and Three Boys."

"That's kind of obvious."

"Kind of Obvious is a cool name."

"Death Demons!"

"The Dunderheads?"

"What does Dunderhead mean?"

"Never mind."

"The Dead Skulls."

"What about The Middle-Schoolers?"

"*That* is the worst name ever."

"You said The Music People was the worst name ever."

"No. Rabbit Attackers is the worst name ever."

"What about The Black Skulls of Death?"

All of the names that had "death" or "skeleton" or "black" or "skull" or "night" in them were Landon's.

Zeke looked over at me. "What about . . . The Bats?"

"No!" I said.

Landon flipped his drumstick in the air and caught it. "Hey, Tom, have you learned how to turn into a bat and fly yet?"

"No."

"You gotta learn how to do that, dude."

"You should try and do it right now," said Zeke, smiling and nodding at me.

I had to change the subject. "Hey, I thought we were going to practice?"

Annie stood up. "Tom's right. Let's worry about our name later and play some music."

18.

Clothes Make the Band

Everybody got their instruments ready to play. I stood by the microphone, next to Annie.

"What are we going to wear when we perform?" asked Capri as she sat down at the piano.

Zeke's eyes lit up. "We should wear capes!"

"We are *not* wearing capes, Zeke," said Annie, strapping on her guitar.

"What about matching hoodies?"

"No!"

"What about different-colored hoodies?"

"Hoodies mess up my hair!" said Capri.

"Let's just wear jeans and T-shirts," said Annie.

"No, I want to wear a dress," said Capri.

"Abel, do you even own a pair of jeans?" asked Landon.

"Yes. I have a pair of vintage, 1955, 501 Levi's, with hidden copper rivets on the back pockets, zinc button fly, made with selvedge denim."

"Hey!" said Zeke. "Why don't we all wear suits and ties, like Abel?"

I remembered something. "Uh, guys, if we ever play outside in the daytime, I have to wear a hat and a long-sleeved shirt and dark glasses."

Annie held up her hands. "Guys! It doesn't matter *what* we wear! It's what we play. C'mon, this is supposed to be a band practice, let's play."

Landon tapped on his one drum. "What kind of music are we gonna do?"

Everybody started talking

"Rap."

"Rock!"

"EDM."

"Hip-hop!"

"Indie Americana Folk"

"What?"

"Techno!"

"Metal!"

"Ew!" said Capri. "I hate metal! I want to do songs from *Frozen*."

"If we do that, I'm gonna throw up!" said Landon.

"I'd like to play some jazz," said Abel. "If that is mutually agreeable with everyone?"

"Jazz is too hard."

"And too boring."

"What kind of music do you want to play, Tom?" asked Annie.

"I don't really care what kind of music we play as long as it makes us rich and famous."

"Yeah!" said Landon. "I want a limo and a private jet!"

"I hope you're joking," said Annie, looking serious. "I want to play good music."

I wasn't joking, but I said I was. "Well, sure, yeah, I want to do good music too. But why can't we also be rich and famous?"

Abel raised his hand. "I would like to suggest that we play a song that Ms. Barstow has written."

Everybody agreed.

Annie pulled some notebook paper out of her guitar case. "I wrote a new song last night."

Just then, her mom poked her head in the door.

"Hey, guys. Time to wrap it up. Capri, your dad's here."

We didn't play one single note of music.

It was The Worst First Band Practice of All Time.

19.

Mad Scientist

"Our band is gonna be excellent!" said Zeke as we walked back to my house.

Not if we never play any music, I thought. But I didn't say anything. I just let Zeke talk for the three blocks back. He talked about his banjo, bats, flying, Martha Livingston, robots, and his skateboard that got stolen last year.

We always thought Tanner Gantt stole it but we could never prove it.

We were almost back to my house when I said, "We gotta decide what we're doing for our science project."

"I still think *you* should be our science project, Bat-Tom."

"I am not going to be a science project!"

We heard an old, crackly voice with a German accent.

"Someone needs to do science project, yah?"

It was Professor Beiersdorfer, the retired science teacher who lived across the street from me.

He was sitting on his front porch in a rocking chair. He had on his usual red sweater, white shirt, tie, black pants, and rubber boots.

Zeke waved. "Hi, Professor Beiersdorfer."

"Ezekiel. The boy who is always in the constant motion. And Thomas. How is our city's one-and-only Blutsauger-Wolf Mann-Zombie?"

"What's a . . . *Blutsauger*?" asked Zeke.

"It is German. It means . . . bloodsucker." He took off his glasses and cleaned them with his handkerchief. "You were talking of a science project, yah? Perhaps I may be of help. I know a thing or two about science."

He laughed without opening his mouth, which was creepy.

"Excellent!" said Zeke. "Do you have any experiments we could do with . . . *robots*?"

I gave Zeke a dirty look. I don't know why I bother anymore. Even when he sees me, it never makes him stop.

The professor raised his big, bushy eyebrows.

"You like the robots?" He put his glasses back on and stood up. "Come tomorrow. After the school. We work in my laboratory. In the basement. Until then . . . auf Wiedersehen." He opened his front door, which creaked, and went inside the house.

"T-Man! If he helps us, we could maybe get first place at the Science Fair!"

Zeke started doing jumping jacks. I didn't stop him. This time, he wasn't wrong.

20.

Changing Looks

That night, I was unloading the dishwasher and setting the table, while Emma stirred a big pot of beef stew in slow motion, so she wouldn't have to help me. Mom was out in the garage, fixing an old cuckoo clock she'd found.

Dad walked in and said, "Behold . . . the new and improved . . . Dad."

Emma turned around and screamed. "Oh my God!"

I looked up and I couldn't believe what I saw.

Dad had shaved off his moustache. He looked

completely different. It was so weird. He had looked exactly the same for the eleven and a half years I'd known him.

He spread his arms out. "It's the *new* me. Dad 2.0."

"And you did this . . . w*hy*?" asked Emma, with a shocked expression on her face.

"Well, I was thinking, Tom changed his look. I thought I'd change my look too."

"Dad, I didn't change my look on purpose. A vampire, a werewolf, and a zombie changed it."

"I know. But you inspired me. And I was getting tired of the moustache."

I think Dad had done it to make me feel better about the way I looked. I guess I'd get used to it, like I'd gotten used to Annie's short hair and glasses.

"So? What do you think?" He moved around the kitchen and did different poses like he was a model. I have to admit: Dad can be funny sometimes. I laughed. Emma tried not to laugh, but she did.

"Parents are supposed to stay the same," said Emma.

"Where does it say that?" said Dad. "You change *your* look, Emma."

"No, I don't!"

This might be the biggest lie Emma has ever told in her life. She changes her look *all the time*. She's had blond hair, brown hair, red hair, and purple hair, short hair, shaved hair, spiky hair, and curly hair. I don't even remember what her real hair looks like.

"Does Mom like it?" asked Emma.

"I love it!" she said, coming in from the garage. "He looks even more handsome."

"Whoa! Let's not get carried away," said Emma.

"Who is this gorgeous man in my kitchen?" she asked, snuggling up to Dad.

Emma shut her eyes. "Stop! No! We just got on The Gross Train and I am derailing it right now. No one wants to see or listen to this."

Emma was right, for once. It is embarrassing to see your parents do stuff like that.

We sat down to eat and I told them about Professor Beiersdorfer offering to help me and Zeke on our science project.

"That's great," said The Man Who Didn't Look Like Dad.

"You couldn't find anyone better," said Mom.

Emma pushed a piece of potato around her plate. "I just hope Professor Beiersdorfer doesn't turn you into a robot."

Dad laughed. Mom didn't.

"Seriously, Tom," said Emma. "I would *not* go into his house if I were you."

"Why not?" I asked.

"Think about it. . . . He's a scientist. You're the world's only Vam-Wolf-Zom. He's going to want to do experiments on you so he can win the Nobel

Prize for science. Then he'll stuff you and put you in a museum."

"Emma, that's ridiculous!" said Mom.

"Is it?" said Emma. "That's what they did to Joseph Merrick, the Elephant Man."

"That's true," said The Man with No Moustache. "But don't worry, Tom, I'd come visit you every single day. Except when the museum was closed."

Emma tried to sound scary. "I guess you'll find out . . . tomorrow."

21.

The Perfect Haunted House

The next day, after school, on Friday, Zeke and I were standing on Professor Beiersdorfer's front porch. His house was the oldest one in town, and it could've used some paint. The big oak door had a metal door knocker on it. I lifted it up and knocked.

Clang. Clang. Clang.

Zeke loved that sound. He wanted to knock again, but I stopped him.

We heard footsteps from inside getting closer. The heavy door slowly opened, making the longest creaking noise ever. Professor Beiersdorfer's craggy face appeared out of the darkness.

"Guten Tag, my fellow scientists."

"Your door makes an *excellent* creaky sound!" said Zeke.

"Yah. I must oil hinges. It is on my list."

"Thanks for helping us, Professor Beiersdorfer," I said.

"Please. Call me Professor B. That way, we waste no time." He raised a finger. "'Do not squander time,

for that is the stuff life is made of.' Your American genius Benjamin Franklin said that."

Zeke blurted out. "Tom knows a girl that knew—"

"A lot of stuff about Ben Franklin," I quickly said. "She helped me with a report."

"Hopefully, I can help you also. Come in."

We went inside and Zeke closed the door slowly, so he could hear the creaky noise again. It was dark and dreary inside. I looked up and saw a dusty crystal chandelier hanging from the ceiling. I think there was a cobweb on it. We peered down a long hallway, with wallpaper that looked like it had little eyes in it, staring at you.

"Professor B, you should do a haunted house in here for Halloween!" said Zeke.

I had to admit he was right. It looked exactly like a haunted house in one of the old black-and-white horror movies that Gram and I watch.

"A haunted house?" said Professor B. "I need to find some ghosts, yah?"

"Yeah!" said Zeke. "Have a séance or get a Ouija board!"

Professor B did that creepy closed-mouth laugh again. "Well, as men of science, we know ghosts do not exist."

Zeke totally believed in ghosts. "They don't?"

"Ezekiel, my boy, think how many cell phones with the cameras there are in the world? Around seven billion. Why is there not one single authentic picture or video of a ghost?"

Zeke scrunched his face up to think. "Well . . . maybe it's because, like, you can't take a picture of Tom, because he's one-third vampire."

Professor B turned to look at me. "This is true?"

I nodded.

"*Very interesting.* We should do experiment about that. Maybe we win Nobel Prize, yah?"

I thought about what Emma had said and did a fake smile.

"Would you gentlemen like something to eat? A strudel? I know zombies have the ravenous appetite, yah?"

"No, thanks," I said. I made sure I'd eaten before we came over.

"Come. We go to laboratory," said Professor B as he padded down the long, dark hallway. "Do you have idea for project?"

"Not really," I said.

"Ideas can come at any time. Sometimes, in middle of night, I get idea and go to lab and work."

We stopped at a door that had a big lock on it. "Here we are."

"Do you have, like, top secret, dangerous stuff in your lab?" asked Zeke.

Professor B smiled. "We shall see."

He unlocked the door with a key he had on a string around his neck. We followed him down some wooden stairs that were even creakier than the front door, to the dark basement.

"Be careful," he said. "I wouldn't want you to have . . . an *accident*."

Why did he say that?

What kind of accident?

Was he going to tell our parents that we tripped going down the stairs? And accidentally fell into a vat of acid he had left open by mistake? And dissolved, and that's why we disappeared? Then he could turn us into robots!

"Hey, T-Man," said Zeke, pointing at a shovel hanging on the wall. "That's the shovel we saw Professor B use when he was burying something in his backyard the night we tried your night vision for the first time."

Why did Zeke have to say that out loud?

Professor B looked sad. "Yah. I had to bury my dear Gretchen."

Who was Gretchen?

His wife? His mother? His sister? His girlfriend? I'd never seen anybody at his house. Had he murdered Gretchen and buried her in his backyard?

"She was my precious kitty cat," he said.

I felt a little bit better.

Then, he switched on a light.

It was a big room with cement floors and walls. In the middle, under a hanging light bulb, was a long, white, metal table, like they do autopsies on. Along one wall there were shelves with glass test tubes and beakers and weird machines with knobs and dials and a really old computer.

It looked like your basic mad scientist's laboratory. The kind where you take brains out of people and reanimate corpses and put animal heads on people's bodies and turn kids into robots.

"This is excellent!" said Zeke.

I was worried he was going to start doing jumping jacks, but he didn't.

Professor Beiersdorfer gestured to piles of books and stacks of papers scattered around.

"Please excuse the mess." Then he tapped the side of his head with his finger. "But the real mess is up here."

Did that mean he was crazy? Or he just had a messy brain?

He pulled a book down from a shelf, blew off some dust, and started flipping through the pages.

"Let us see now. What is the good science project? Something with acid? . . . Nitroglycerin? . . . Volcanoes?"

I looked across the room and saw a shelf that had little cages with animals in them. I could hear them moving. I walked over to the cages to get a better look. He had a black hamster, a brown guinea pig—and a mouse who looked very familiar.

"Terrence?"

22.

The Reunion

The mouse looked up at me. It *was* Terrence. I could tell he recognized me because he started shaking and backed away to the corner of his cage.

"Where'd you get your mouse, Professor?" I asked.

"Otto? Very interesting story. I was taking the trash out. I look down. There is Otto. On the curb. Shaking. Quivering. Why? I do not know."

I knew. I'd swallowed him and then thrown him up. I'd be shaking and quivering too. I didn't say anything. Terrence was much better off living here. His cage was clean, he had plenty of food and water, and nobody was going to try to eat him again. And Otto was a much better name than Terrence.

Just to be safe, I asked, "You're not doing any experiments where you try to make these animals giant, are you?"

Professor Beiersdorfer chuckled. "Like Godzilla?" He shook his head. "No. No monsters. And no experiments. They are my friends. They keep me company while I work."

I was glad to hear that.

"So, Thomas," said Professor B. "How are you coping with your . . . *condition*?"

"Fine."

That's what I usually say when people ask me how I am. It's the best thing to say to adults, otherwise you might get in a long, boring conversation.

"I told Tom that *he* should be our science project," said Zeke, for the millionth time.

Professor B nodded. "You would be *very* interesting project."

"See! I told you!" said Zeke.

"Have you transformed yet, Thomas? Made yourself into the bat? Tried to fly?"

I could see Zeke, behind Professor B, mouthing the word: *Yes! Yes! Yes!*

"I tried," I said. That was the truth. I didn't have to tell him I succeeded.

Professor B sighed. "To fly would be . . . wunderbar."

Zeke went over to a long, narrow, wooden box in the corner.

"Is this a *coffin*?"

Professor B chuckled. "No. It is seismograph. For recording earthquake activity. I show you."

I knew Zeke wished it was a coffin. Professor B opened the lid, which also creaked, and showed Zeke how it worked. I saw a notebook on the shelf next to Terrence's cage. I figured it must be notes on one of his experiments. I leaned over to read it. Since it was open, I wasn't technically spying.

Dear Diary,

Robot experiment XL-5.

Today I will try to turn a boy into a robot. It can work! It must work! No one can stop me! I just need two boys to start! Maybe some kids from the neighborhood will do?

For the first time in her life Emma was right. Professor Beiersdorfer really *was* a mad scientist and he wanted to turn kids into robots.

"Zeke!" I shouted, moving toward the stairs. "I-I forgot something! We gotta go!"

"What? We do? Why?"

"We gotta go to . . . to . . . uh—that thing!"

"What thing?" Zeke just stood there. He *never* stands in one place, but today, for some reason, he did.

"The party!" I said.

"What party?"

"Uh . . . Tanner Gantt's birthday party! Come on!"

"Tanner Gantt is having a birthday party?"

Zeke was even more confused than usual. Tanner Gantt would *never* invite us to his birthday party. But it was the first thing I thought of and luckily, Zeke believes almost everything I tell him.

"You must go?" asked Professor B. "So soon?"

"Yeah! Sorry! Come on, Zeke! Hurry up!"

Zeke has never moved slower in his life than he did walking toward the stairs.

"T-Man, that's so weird that Tanner Gantt invited us. I hope they have ice cream cake."

"What about science project?" said Professor B, standing by the wooden box that probably *was* a coffin.

"Oh, yeah, uh, I forgot," I said. "I already made a project."

"You did?" said Zeke.

"What is it?" asked Professor Beiersdorfer.

"It's . . . uh . . . called 'Can Ants Escape from an Ant Farm?'"

"I thought you said you didn't want to do that?" said Zeke as I pushed him up the creaky stairs.

"I changed my mind!"

"Excellent!"

"Thanks anyway, Professor B!" I said at the top of the stairs.

I pushed Zeke down the dark hall and out the creaky front door. We ran across the street to my house. When we got inside, I slammed the door shut.

"Don't slam the door!" yelled Dad from somewhere.

"Sorry!" I yelled back.

Zeke and I leaned against the front door and caught our breath.

"T-Man . . . what are we . . . gonna get . . . Tanner Gantt . . . for his birthday?"

"Zeke . . . there's no . . . birthday party."

"There isn't? Aw, man."

He was disappointed, like I knew he would be. I told him about what I read in Professor B's notebook.

"He really wants to turn us into robots?!" said Zeke.

"Yeah. Emma was right."

"A robot army would be awesome!"

"Not if *we're* the robot army!"

"But what if we were, like, cool robots, that could shoot fire from our eyes and rockets from our mouths and fly?"

"Zeke, we *don't* want to be robots!"

"Yeah, I guess. Should we call the police, T-Man?"

"They wouldn't believe us. We'd have to show them the notebook."

"We gotta steal it," said Zeke."To prove it."

"How are we going to get into his lab?"

"You can turn into a bat, sneak inside, and get it!"

Sometimes I forget I can do stuff like that.

Get Professor Beiersdorfer's Notebook Plan

1. Wait until Professor B goes to bed

2. Turn into a bat

3. Sneak into his laboratory

4. Get notebook!

5. Show notebook to police

"Mom, can Zeke spend the night?"

She looked up from the old dollhouse she was painting in the garage.

"If it's okay with his mom, it's okay with me."

I grabbed a pair of binoculars from the shelf.

"Who are you going to spy on?" she said suspiciously.

"Nobody. It's for a school assignment."

"Okay," she said.

As long as you say something is for school, you can pretty much get your parents to let you use anything.

० ० ०

From my bedroom window we had a perfect view of Professor B's house. Zeke watched him through the binoculars.

"Suspect is in his living room, T-Man, sitting in a chair, reading a book."

"I know, Zeke, I can see him. I have night vision."

"Copy that, T-Man!"

"Can you see what book he's reading?"

"Negative. It's probably *How to Make Kids into Robots*— Wait! I can see it. Suspect is reading . . . I don't know. The title's in German, I think."

I looked through the binoculars: *Charlie und die Schokoladenfabrik.*

We translated it on my computer. *Charlie and the Chocolate Factory.*

We looked at each other.

"Why's he reading that?" asked Zeke.

"I don't know. . . . That's bizarre."

"Do you have any chocolate up here, T-Man?"

"No."

"Does Emma?"

"I don't know."

"Does your mom have some in the kitchen?"

"Focus, Zeke!"

o o o

We pretended to be asleep at eleven o'clock, when my mom checked on us. I'm good at doing that, but Zeke does the worst fake snore ever.

"Nice snoring, Zeke," said my mom.

"Thanks, Mrs. Marks!" said Zeke, from his sleeping bag on the floor.

"Don't stay up too late." She closed the door.

We went back to the window. At eleven

fifteen, Professor B yawned, closed his book, and went upstairs. The light went on in his bedroom. Thankfully he went into the bathroom to get into his pajamas. Then he got into bed, and turned out the light.

Zeke lowered the binoculars and turned to me. "Commence Operation: Steal Notebook."

23.

Code Red

As we went downstairs and snuck out the back door, Zeke started singing.

"Da, da, dum-dum! Da, da, dum-dum! Da—"

"What are you doing?!"

"It's our spy theme song"

"Zeke, real spies don't sing theme songs."

"I know. But in movies they always have cool music."

"Just be quiet."

"Okay, T-Man," he said as we crossed the street to Professor B's house.

"Did you make up that song?"

"Yeah."

I have to admit, it was a pretty good spy song.

First, we had to figure out how to get in. We walk-ed around the whole house, but all the windows were shut tight.

"How are you going to get in, Bat-Tom? Chimney? Air vent?"

I looked at the front door.

"Mail slot."

We quietly crept up to the front porch, and Zeke lifted up the mail slot in the front door.

"I'll go in, go down to the lab, and get the notebook," I said. "Then, I'll open a window and pass it out to you."

Zeke saluted.

I made sure no one was watching us and said, "Turn to bat. Bat, I shall be."

I turned into a bat, slipped in through the mail slot, and landed on the floor. The hallway looked even scarier at night with all the dark shadows.

"Good luck, Bat-Tom," said Zeke, peeking through the mail slot. "I'll keep an eye on the suspect from the front lawn. Over and out!"

I flew down the hallway to the locked lab. I had to squeeze in under the door. It was tight, but I made it.

I hopped down the stairs. The basement lab was like the set of a horror movie, especially with my black-and-white night vision. You'd think because I'm a monster—well, technically three monsters—that stuff like that wouldn't be scary. I have to admit it was.

"Turn to human. Human, I shall be."

I walked over to the shelf where I'd seen the notebook, by Terrence's cage. He was asleep and so was the guinea pig. The hamster was awake, watching me.

The notebook wasn't there.

Had Professor B hidden it?

Destroyed it?

Locked it up in a safe?

If we couldn't get the notebook, people would think we were crazy. I looked on the other shelves and tables, but it was nowhere. I was about to give up when I saw the long seismograph box that maybe was a coffin. The notebook was on top.

Bam! Bam! Bam!

I turned around and saw Zeke banging on the window.

"Bat-Tom! Code Red! Repeat: Code Red! Suspect is awake and on the move! This is not a drill!"

I heard Professor B's footsteps right above me. He went down the hallway and stopped at the door to the lab. Then a key turned in the lock, and the door at the top of the stairs opened. He was coming down.

"Turn to bat! Bat, I shall be!" I whispered.

I flew over to the shelf and landed between Terrence's and the guinea pig's cages. Terrence woke up, saw me, and started making those loud, high-pitched mouse noises.

"Terrence! Shh! Shut up!"

I wished Emma had trained him. Can you train mice?

The light went on and Professor B came down the creaky stairs. He was whistling. It was one of those creepy nursery-rhyme songs that you hear in scary movies just before somebody gets killed.

Terrence, The World's Nosiest Mouse, kept squeaking and freaking out. The guinea pig and hamster didn't make a sound.

"Otto?" said Professor B when he got to the bottom of the stairs.

He was walking right toward me, so I slid behind the guinea pig's cage, against the wall where it was dark, and hoped he wouldn't see me.

Professor B bent down and looked in Otto's cage.

"Otto? What is wrong, Liebling?"

I figured I had two options:

1. Stay hidden and hope he didn't see me.
2. Fly out across the lab, up the stairs, down the hallway, and out through the mail slot. Hopefully, he'd think I was a real bat that had gotten into his basement.

I went with #1. I curled myself up into the tiniest ball I could, wrapping my wings around me. I squeezed my big bat eyes shut, so he wouldn't see them. Why was he down here? He must have had some stupid scientific idea.

Then, I felt a warm hand wrap around me.

"Hello, little bat," Professor B said, picking me up.

I tried to wriggle away, but I couldn't get out. This is what Martha Livingston must have felt when I grabbed her.

"How did you get in here? You must be smart bat, yah?"

Should I bite him? No. Then he might turn into a vampire if our blood accidentally mixed together.

Should I talk and tell him who I was? No. He might get mad because I'd snuck into his house.

"I think I keep you a little while. Study you for a few days."

He put me in a cage on the edge of the shelf and locked the little door.

I was Professor Beiersdorfer's pet bat.

24.

The Worst Idea Ever

Professor B rubbed his chin and started talking to himself.

"Beiersdorfer, you dummkopf, what did you come down for?" He hit his forehead with his hand. "Yah! Now I remember!"

He went over to the seismograph box, picked up the notebook, and walked back to the stairs.

"Guten Nacht, Otto, and my new little bat. I shall name you Max." He stopped at the bottom of the stairs and turned around. "Or maybe you should be named Heidi? We find out tomorrow."

I had to get out of there.

He went up the creaky stairs, turned out the light, and I heard the door close.

I tried to unlock my cage door, but I didn't have fingers, just stupid bat wings, which were useless. I tried to use my bat feet, but they were too tiny. There was only one thing I could do. I had to turn back into a human and bust out of the cage. I had no idea what was going to happen.

I kept throwing my bat body against the side of the cage to move it, inch by inch, toward the edge of the shelf. The cage finally tipped off the edge and clanged onto the floor. I hoped this wasn't a big mistake. I closed my eyes.

"Turn to human. Human, I shall be."

BAM!

I turned back to me as the cage broke apart and fell into little pieces on the floor. Terrence started freaking out again.

I unlocked the basement window, opened it, and yelled.

"Zeke! Zeke!"

He ran over and bent down on the grass.

"Talk to me, T-Man!"

"He took the notebook."

"I know! I just saw suspect return to bedroom with it. Abort the mission?"

"No! I'll go upstairs and get it."

Zeke saluted. "See you on the other side, Bat-Tom."

o o o

I closed and locked the basement window so Professor B wouldn't know someone had been in there. Then I turned into a bat again. I squeezed under the lab door at the top of the stairs, and flew down the hallway and upstairs to the second floor. I could tell which room was his bedroom because I could hear him snoring. It actually sounded like Zeke's fake snoring.

I peeked in the open doorway.

He was asleep in bed, with the notebook in one hand and a pencil in the other. He must have fallen asleep while writing. I decided to turn back into me, because I wasn't sure I could pick up the notebook with my bat feet. I whispered, "Turn to human. Human, I shall be."

I tiptoed into the room. I went up to the bed and slowly, carefully slid the notebook out of his hand. He stopped snoring and I froze. What would I say if he woke up.

"Hi, Professor B. I can turn into a bat. Want to see?"

Luckily, he stayed asleep. I went over to the window, quietly opened it, and tossed the notebook down to Zeke, who caught it and gave me a thumbs-up.

I went downstairs to the front door and said, "Turn to bat. Bat, I shall be." I went through the mail slot and turned back into me. It was pretty cool that we'd pulled it off. As we ran across the street to my house, I almost started singing Zeke's spy song.

о о о

We went in my bedroom, and I opened the notebook to show Zeke the page I had read in the lab.

"'Dear Diary, Robot experiment XL-5. Today I will try to turn a boy into a robot.'"

"Excellent!" said Zeke. "Do you think he'd let us pick our robot color? I'd wanna be silver! What would my robot name be? Robo-Zeke? The Zeke-Bot? The Zeke-Anator?"

"This is not a good thing, Zeke!"

He turned the page and made a weird face. "Why does it say 'Ideas for Book'?"

"What?"

He showed me.

IDEAS FOR BOOK

- Kid survives on the moon with only a toothbrush.
- Girl saves a baby unicorn from being sold to a circus in Salzburg.
- Boy trades his parents for video game.
- Mermaid joins school swim team.
- Boy puts on magical lederhosen and can fly.
- Mad scientist makes giant pretzel that comes alive and takes over the world.
- Mad scientist makes two boys into robots.

"It's a book," I said. "Professor B is writing a book about a mad scientist who turns kids into robots. He's not really going to do it."

Stealing the notebook was the WORST idea Zeke and I had ever had.

And now I had to put
it back in his bedroom
before Professor B
noticed it was
gone.

We went back to his house. I changed into a bat,
went in the mail slot, turned back to me, got the
notebook from Zeke through the slot, went upstairs,
put the notebook next to Professor B's hand, went
back downstairs, turned into a bat, went through
the slot, turned back to me, and went home.

Being a spy in real life is much harder than it is
in the movies.

Plus, Zeke and I still had a problem.

What to do for our science project?

25.

To Fly or Not to Fly

Ladies and gentlemen, Tom Marks, the Vam-Wolf-Zom! We have been studying and performing various experiments on this fascinating person, who is also my best friend," said Zeke.

It was three days later and we were in the gym. I stood in front of a cardboard chart that showed pictures of different kinds of food and a bat. Zeke was next to me, holding a pointer stick. There were science projects set up all around the gym. Annie, Abel, and Landon had projects too.

"What is a Vam-Wolf-Zom's favorite food and

drink?" said Zeke. "After studying Tom, we discovered it was meat and blood."

I glanced over at Mr. Prady, who didn't look like he was going to give us first place. Or even thirty-first.

"How strong is a Vam-Wolf-Zom?" said Zeke.

I picked Zeke up and held him over my head.

"Our conclusion: Strong!" said Zeke as I set him back down. "And last, but not least: Can a Vam-Wolf-Zom turn into a bat and fly?" said Zeke. "We will prove today, before your very eyes, whether this can happen or not."

Mr. Prady started to look interested. The other kids in the gym were crowding around. I could tell they were expecting me to do it.

"Let us find out!" Zeke turned to me. "Mr. Marks . . . can you turn into a bat and fly!"

I knew I could do it. I'd done it lots of times, but only alone or in front of Zeke. I looked up at how high the ceiling was in the gym. I could fly around in circles a few times and land back where our project was. It might get us first place.

I looked out at all those eyes staring at me. I saw Annie smiling at me. Even Tanner Gantt, who didn't do a project, was standing there with his arms crossed, smirking.

I started to get nervous. I didn't want to do a crash landing and have everybody laugh at me. I slowly shook my head.

Zeke nodded and turned to face everyone. "And so, our scientific conclusion is: Negative. A Vam-Wolf-Zom cannot turn into a bat and fly."

I heard Tanner say, "Lame!"

Zeke bowed. Why did he always bow? You could tell all the kids were really disappointed that I didn't fly. And so was Mr. Prady. He gave us thirty-second place. I blame Zeke for coming up with the idea, Professor Beiersdorfer for not giving us a better one, Martha Livingston for turning me, the werewolf, and the zombie guy too.

○ ○ ○

Annie got third place for her project, "Does Music Affect Brain Waves?" Abel got tenth place for "How

Does Water Affect Cotton, Linen, and Corduroy?" Landon even got a higher score than us, thirty-first place, for his project, "Telekinesis: Can You Move a Penny with Your Mind?" He just sat there and stared at a penny for five minutes. It never moved. But he had a big chart with lots of pictures and numbers.

Landon came up to me, afterward, in the hallway. "Can I use your dad's drum set?"

"Yeah, Landon."

"Hey, don't call me Landon anymore, call me Dog Hots."

"What? You said not to."

"I changed my mind."

"Why?"

Just then, two eighth-grade girls walked by. They were pretty, but they didn't look nice.

"Hey, Dog Hots!" said one.

"How's it going, Dog Hots?" said the other.

Landon smiled and said, "Awesome, ladies!"

The girls walked off covering their mouths with their hands and giggling.

"See!" he said, turning to me. "They think Dog Hots is a cool name."

"Um . . . I don't know about that."

"Hey, you saw it! Eighth-grade girls are talking to me!"

I decided not to spoil his illusion.

He was Dog Hots again.

° ° °

I kept practicing flying and landing every night. I wished they had bat flying and landing lessons on the internet. They have videos on practically everything else. But you can't film a vampire, so it wouldn't work.

A few days after the science fair, I got home from school and Emma said she had a big announcement. She made all of us sit down at the kitchen table.

"What is it, Emma?" asked Mom, who had her worried face on.

"Lucas is coming over to study tonight and stay for dinner."

"I'll alert the media!" said Dad. Mom laughed. Emma didn't.

"Listen to me, very carefully," she said. "Do not ask him stupid questions. Mom, do not show him the weird stuff you sell in the garage. Dad, do not try to be funny. Tom, do you have to be here?"

"I live here!"

"Can't you go over to Zeke's house? Or stay in your room? Or the basement?"

"No!"

She tried to bribe me. "I'll give you five dollars if you go away."

"Yeah, right! And you'll call that my birthday present. No way!"

"Ten dollars?"

I wondered how high she would go. I might make some serious cash.

"No!" said Mom. "Emma, you are *not* paying your brother to go away."

Emma let out a gigantic sigh.

"All right. Come in. Say 'hi.' And then go away. And, if any of you call him Carrot Boy, I will kill you!"

"Emma," I reminded her. "*You're* the one who came up with the name Carrot Boy, when he used to mow our lawn."

"That's beside the point!"

"Can we call him C.B.?" asked Dad.

"No!"

"Can we call him Mr. C?" I asked.

"No!!"

"The C-Man?" asked Dad.

"NO!!!"

"What about The Boy Who Shall Not Be Named Carrot?" I asked.

"NO!!!!!!"

Ding-dong.

"Someone is at the door!" said Dad. "Who on earth could it be?"

Emma stood up. "Do NOT embarrass me!"

I stood up and saluted. So did Dad. Mom didn't.

26.

Carrot Boy Meets the Vam-Wolf-Zom

Mom, Dad, and I stayed in the kitchen while Emma went to get the door. She let Carrot Boy in, and I could hear them whispering.

"Meet my parents for, like, five seconds and then we'll go study," whispered Emma.

"Why are we whispering?" said Carrot Boy.

"So Tom doesn't hear us. He has super hearing."

"Cool!" said Carrot Boy.

"No, it's not!" said Emma.

Dad turned to Mom. "Let's go meet the new-and-improved Lucas."

He and Mom went into the living room. I stayed in the kitchen and listened.

"Hi, Lucas," said Mom. "Nice to see you again."

"Hey, Mr. and Mrs. Marks," said Carrot Boy.

"Want to mow the lawn for old times' sake?" asked Dad.

I could feel Emma cringing, even from the other room.

Carrot Boy laughed. "No, Mr. Marks. My mowing days are over. I found out I'm allergic to grass. Where's Tom?"

"I don't know," said Emma. "C'mon, let's go study." Emma had never said that in her entire life.

"But I want to meet him."

"Why?" she asked.

"*Why*? 'Cause he's awesome."

"Let me assure you. Tom is not awesome. He is the opposite of awesome."

Mom and Dad went off to do some Mom and Dad stuff, and I went into the living room.

"Hey," I said.

"Hey, Tom," said Carrot Boy. He turned to Emma. "He doesn't look that bad, Emmers."

Emmers?

He turned back to me and smiled. "Dude, I thought you'd be, like, all, you know, messed up, monster freaky, you know what I'm saying? You are rockin' the Vam-Wolf-Zom look."

I shrugged. "Yeah, Emma likes to exaggerate."

"*Dude!* I know! She totally does!"

"I do not!" said Emma, The World's Biggest Exaggerator.

Carrot Boy went on. "And she makes stuff up, like, all the time."

"No, I don't! C'mon, we have to go study, Lukey."

Lukey?

If Annie Barstow decides to be my girlfriend in high school, I'm going to tell her that we can't call each other by lame nicknames.

When we sat down to dinner, I brought a bowl of carrots to the table. I had to. If I hadn't, it would have been the greatest missed opportunity of all time.

"Carrots anybody?" I asked.

Emma gave me a laser-beam death ray with her eyes.

"Yes! I love carrots!" said Carrot Boy.

I couldn't believe he actually said that. I saw Dad bite his lip, so he wouldn't laugh. Even Mom put her hand in front of her mouth to hide her smile.

But I have to admit, Carrot Boy wasn't as bad as I thought he was going to be. And he was the first person who didn't ask me if I could turn into a bat and fly.

27.

Werewolf Time

Can you guys practice this Friday night?" asked Annie.

We were having a band meeting at lunch in the cafeteria a week after The Carrot Boy Dinner.

Abel, Capri, Dog Hots, and Zeke all said yes.

"Um . . . I can't," I said.

Annie crossed her arms. "Why not?"

"There's going to be a full moon."

"So?" she said.

Did she forget I was one-third werewolf?

"I turn into a werewolf, Annie."

She shrugged. "I have no problem with you being a werewolf. We need to practice."

"Excellent!" said Zeke. "I haven't seen you as a werewolf yet!"

"I want to see you go all werewolf!" said Dog Hots.

Abel straightened his tie and tucked his napkin into his collar. "I'm quite intrigued to see you in werewolf state, with your permission of course."

So far, I had only turned into a full-on werewolf three times. The first time was at my house, when I got Mom, Dad, and Emma to believe I was a Vam-Wolf-Zom. The second time was the next night, when we had to convince Principal Gonzales and Mayor Lao. And the third time was the night after that, at Gram's house. There were only two full moons in October, coming up on a Thursday and Friday.

"So, what happens exactly?" asked Capri.

"Well, I get really, really, hairy all over my body. My hands and feet turn into paws. I couldn't see my face, but my nose felt like a snout and my teeth got a little bigger. And I howl sometimes."

Annie frowned. "Try not to howl when we're singing."

○ ○ ○

On the night before band practice, I was in the living room, on the sofa, reading our second book for English. It was about this kid who gets stuck in the woods with a hatchet. I looked out the window as the moon rose, and I turned into a werewolf.

"Ahwooo!"

"Mom!" Emma yelled from the dining room. "Tell Tom to stop howling! I am trying to do homework!"

"She's not doing homework," I yelled. "She's texting Carrot Boy!"

"Don't call him Carrot Boy!" said Emma.

"Tom, please don't howl," said Mom, from the kitchen.

"I'm a werewolf, it's a full moon, I can't help it!"

"Well, try not to howl so loudly," said Mom.

I tried.

"Ahwooo!"

I couldn't.

I got up and started pacing back and forth.

"Someone needs to take wolf-boy for a walk!" said Emma.

"Mom, can I go run around outside for a while?" I asked.

She came into the living room. "It's pretty late. I don't like you going out at night alone."

"Seriously?" said Emma. "He has *claws* and *fangs*. He can *lift up a car*! He can take of himself."

"Okay, Tom, but put on your brown jacket," said Mom.

"I'm covered in fur. I don't need a jacket."

"But you look so nice in it."

"Mom!"

"Okay, okay, never mind."

Dad yelled from the kitchen, "Take Muffin with you. He hasn't been walked."

When I first turned into a Vam-Wolf-Zom, Muffin acted afraid of me. But I guess he was getting used to it. In fact, it seemed like Muffin liked me more when I was a werewolf.

"Come on, Muffin."

He trotted over and I put the leash on him before we headed out the front door.

"Don't eat anybody!" said Emma.

o o o

Professor Beiersdorfer was on his porch in his rocking chair. I hadn't seen him since Operation: Steal Notebook.

"Guten Nacht, Thomas. You are the werewolf tonight, yah?"

"Ahwoooooo!" I couldn't help howling.

"Come close so I may see, please?" he asked.

I went up on the porch and he looked at me. "Very interesting. Excellent example of a lycanthrope."

"A what?" I asked.

"Lycanthrope. Another name for werewolf. From the Greek 'lykos' for wolf and 'anthropos' for man. So? How did science project work out?"

"Not so good. We should've had you help us."

"Next year, perhaps?"

I wanted to ask him about the robot book, but

I couldn't let him know I knew about it, so I said,
"Have you ever written any books, Professor?"

"Yah. Some science books."

"Any other kind?"

He smiled. "I tried to write a book for children.

I used to see you and Ezekiel play robot when you were little. It gave me idea."

That was true. When we were kids, Zeke and I made robot suits out of cardboard boxes and had awesome robot wars on my front lawn. I have to admit, I sort of missed doing stuff like that. I bet Zeke would do it if I asked him.

Professor B said, "Very hard to write good children's book. I read excellent book by Roald Dahl to try to learn. *Charles und Chocolate Factory.*"

That's why he was reading that the other night! Now it all made sense.

"Science book easier to write for me," he said. "So, I give up robot book."

"You should finish it, Professor. I'd read it."

"Maybe. Or maybe I write about Blutsauger-Wolf Mann-Zombie across the street, yah?" He stood up. "Auf Wiedersehen, Thomas."

o o o

Muffin and I walked toward the park. Half a block away, with my night vision, I saw Tanner Gantt sitting by himself on the swings. I'd seen him there before. I cocked my ear to listen. He was humming to himself. I didn't want him to see me, so I turned around and went the other way.

It started to rain, but it didn't bother me because of my fur. As soon as we walked in the house, Emma said, "Ew! You both smell like wet dog! Yet another disgusting thing I have to put up with!"

I growled at her.

So did Muffin.

Emma growled back.

28.

Werewolf Rehearsal

The next night, Friday, I had already turned into a werewolf by the time I got to Annie's house for band practice. It was weird to stand in her living room with my friends staring at me.

"Excellent!" said Zeke, as usual.

"You are *definitely* a werewolf," said Annie.

"Outstanding coat of fur, Mr. Marks," said Abel. "Marvelous pigment and coloration."

"Does it itch?" asked Dog Hots.

"No."

"Can I touch your arm?" asked Annie.

"Sure."

"Wow. That's really soft."

I didn't mind Annie petting my arm.

"Don't you want to touch it, Capri?" she asked.

Capri made a face. "Uh . . . no thanks. Maybe next time."

Everyone touched me except Capri. Which was weird, because she was the one who had asked about seeing me as a werewolf.

"You should've taken a video of yourself getting all hairy," said Dog Hots.

"You can't take a video of me, remember— Wait. Hey, Capri, could you draw a picture of me, so I know what I look like when I'm a werewolf?"

She sighed. "Are you going to tell me how to draw it?"

"No. I promise."

"Aren't we going to practice?" said Annie.

"I'll just do a quick pencil sketch while you guys set up your amps and stuff," said Capri.

They set up the equipment and I posed for Capri. I didn't say anything the whole time she was drawing, so she wouldn't yell at me. She handed me the picture. Annie was right. I *definitely* looked like a werewolf. If I saw someone who looked like me, I'd probably run away. Like Martha told me to do if I ever saw Darcourt the werewolf.

∘ ∘ ∘

Annie played us a new song she'd written. It was about whales or dolphins or porpoises. I wasn't listening very closely, because I was looking at Capri's drawing of my werewolf face.

After finishing, Annie said, "Okay, Tom, this time, sing with me on the chorus."

She played the song again and I started to sing along with her.

"Ahwoooo!"

Annie stopped playing.

"Don't howl, Tom."

"Sorry."

We sang it again.

"Ahwooooooo!"

"Can you *please* not howl, Tom?"

"Sorry. I'm not doing it on purpose. I promise."

We sang it again.

"Ahwooooooooooo!"

Annie stopped playing her guitar. "Tom!"

"I can't help it!"

"Try!"

I tried not to howl, but I couldn't stop.

"Maybe we should do this song when I'm not a werewolf?" I suggested.

"I agree," said Annie.

"Let's do something that rocks!" said Dog Hots. He started pounding out the beat to "We Will Rock You" by that old band Queen on his snare drum. Everybody else stomped their feet and clapped.

As I soon as I started singing the words, everybody turned around and looked at me.

My voice sounded amazing. It was deeper, rougher, louder, and more powerful. I sounded older too.

"That was awesome!" said Dog Hots.

"Mega-excellent!" said Zeke.

Capri smiled. "Wow."

"Astonishing change in your vocal quality," said Abel.

"I'll have to write a song for you," said Annie.

Maybe our band *would* get famous! Maybe we'd tour all over the world! Have millions of fans! Make millions of dollars!

"Do you think it's because you're a werewolf?" asked Annie.

I hadn't thought of that.

The next morning, when I woke up, I sang in the shower.

My older, deeper, rougher, lower voice was gone.

I guess I could only sing like that when there was a full moon. Why isn't anything ever one hundred percent perfect?

29.

The Invisible Vam-Wolf-Zom

Halloween was coming up. I love Halloween. It's one of the best holidays ever invented. I rank it #3 on my list of Top-Ten Best Holidays.

Tom Marks's Top-Ten Best Holidays
(And Why)

#1. Christmas: I get presents and a two-week vacation. No contest, this is my favorite holiday.

#2. My Birthday: Presents. Not as many as at Christmas, but they are all for me. (Technically it's not really a holiday, but it's my list, so I can put it here.)

#3. Halloween: Free candy. I get to dress up as somebody else and scare people without getting in trouble.

#4. Easter/Spring Break: I get a whole week off from school, and some candy.

#5. Thanksgiving: It's mostly about food, but I do get two days off from school.

#6. Tie between Veterans Day, Memorial Day, Martin Luther King Day, and Presidents' Day: I get one day off from school for each of them. They should also give us a day off for Benjamin Franklin's birthday. He did a lot of amazing things. But I wish he'd been a better fighter and had beaten up that vampire Lovick Zabrecky so he didn't bite Martha Livingston.

#7. Labor Day: I don't really know what it's for. Something about people who work. I get one day off from school.

#8. The Fourth of July: Fireworks and barbecued hot dogs and hamburgers. It's during summer vacation, so I'm not in school.

#9. Valentine's Day: Some candy, but not the good kind. It can be embarrassing if you don't get a lot of valentines. I still have to go to school.

#10. St. Patrick's Day: I liked it when I was little and we hunted for the leprechaun's treasure at school and got chocolate gold coins. Mom makes corned beef and cabbage, which I don't like. But maybe I will now, since I'm a Vam-Wolf-Zom and like any type of meat.

For some reason I had never dressed up as a vampire or a werewolf or a zombie for Halloween when I was a kid. Now I'm all three, whether I want to be or not. I'm a Halloween character *every single day of the year.*

30.

No Costume, No Candy

The main reason I was looking forward to Halloween was because I could wear a mask and a costume and *nobody* would know who I was when I went trick-or-treating. People wouldn't point at me or stare or whisper, "That's the Vam-Wolf-Zom kid!"

You can't wear a mask at school, so everyone would know who I was there. I decided to wear one costume to school on Friday and the dance that night, and a different costume, with a mask, when I went trick-or-treating.

Some middle-school kids think they're too cool to go trick-or-treating. They're crazy! Why wouldn't you want to go out and get tons of free candy? I'm going to go trick-or-treating for as long as I can, in high school and maybe even college. And I'm always going to wear a costume. It bugs me when people don't dress up and still want candy. When I grow up and have a house, I'm not going to give any candy to people if they're not dressed up. I'm going to put a sign on my front door.

I won't care how old you are, as long as you're in a costume, you get candy.

I *really* hate those T-shirts that say "This Is My Halloween Costume." That is *not* a costume. No candy for anyone wearing those.

And kids have to say "Trick or Treat" too. They can't just stand there and hold their bags out. I hate it when kids don't say "Trick or Treat."

Two weeks before Halloween, I was walking down the hallway to first period and I could smell Tanner Gantt coming up behind me. He smelled like Cheetos as usual.

"So, what are you gonna be for Halloween, Freak Face? Oh, right! I forgot: You don't have to put on a mask, you can just come as you are!"

I didn't say anything to him. Tanner Gantt doesn't do Halloween. I'd never seen him go out trick-or-treating. He stands on a corner and makes kids give him their candy by threatening to beat them up, or he steals candy from kids when they bring it to school the next day.

I went into English and sat down at my desk away from the window. All the teachers let me sit away from the windows so the sun doesn't shine on me. After the bell rang and Mr. Kessler took roll, there was an announcement on the loudspeaker.

"Good morning, this is Principal Gonzales. Halloween is coming up and I wanted to go over the rules about costumes at school. You may wear them during the day, when we have our costume contest, and for the dance in the gym that evening. These rules will be in a handout sent to your parents."

He cleared his throat and went on.

"Costumes may not demean or make fun of any group or individual. No inappropriate or revealing costumes, such as skimpy pajamas or bathing suits."

Who would want to wear a bathing suit to school?

"Costumes may not show obscene materials or threats. No prohibited substances or paraphernalia. No masks allowed."

"Boo," said a kid in class.

"Quiet," said Mr. Kessler.

"Makeup is allowed, but nothing offensive, and the student's face must be visible at all times. No canes. No sticks. No weapon-like items, and that includes lightsabers, all you Jedi Knights. They *will* be confiscated. No excessive blood."

Some kids in the class grumbled.

"Settle down," said Mr. Kessler.

Principal Gonzales went on. "Also, this year we have added a new rule."

What *else* couldn't we do?

"This year there can be no vampire . . . no werewolf . . . and no zombie costumes. Thank you. Have a happy Halloween!"

The whole class went crazy.

"That sucks!"

"I already made my zombie costume!"

"No fair!"

"I just bought a werewolf makeup kit!"

"Marks, you owe me thirty-five dollars!"

"My mom made me a vampire cape!"

"That's unconstitutional!" (That was Annie.)

"Thanks for ruining Halloween, Marks!"

"I'm suing the school!"

"Knock it off!" said Mr. Kessler. "Look, maybe some of you will have to be more creative this year. Come up with something new and different, so I won't have to see the same costumes I see every single year when I judge the contest. Personally, I'm tired of vampires, werewolves, and zombies." Then he looked at me and said, "Not that there's anything wrong with them."

I got a lot of dirty looks from kids the rest of the day.

It wasn't my fault I got bit by a vampire and a werewolf and a zombie. Why didn't anybody understand that?

31.

The Randee Rabbit Problem

I had two weeks to decide what I should wear
to school and what I'd wear to trick or treat. And I
had to deal with Zeke's Halloween costume.

Zeke has worn the same costume for the past
three years. He dresses up as Randee Rabbit. It's a
character in Rabbit Attack!, which is also known
as The Worst Video Game Ever. Zeke plays it every
day. I am not kidding.

Zeke made me buy Rabbit Attack! before I had
played it. Big mistake. I played it one time, and it
was horrible. He's always trying to get me to play

it with him, but I refuse. Once was enough. I was so mad after I played it that one time, I actually wrote a letter to the creators.

Dear Machine-Box Video Games,

Rabbit Attack! is the worst video game I have ever played. Why would you make such a boring game? Who wants a game where rabbits just throw carrots back and forth at each other? I used my allowance money from three months to buy it. I would like my money back, or a better game. Death Bomb Massacre or World War Ten look good.

A very unhappy customer,

Thomas Marks

Two weeks later I got a letter from them in the mail.

Dear Thomas Marks,

We are very sorry you did not like Rabbit Attack! Unfortunately we cannot refund your money, or send you another game, but we are enclosing some Rabbit Attack! stickers.

Keep Gaming!

Ms. Kristy Randall, Customer Service

P.S. Try throwing some carrots down the rabbit hole.

STRENGTH

DEXTERITY

RANDEE RABBIT

I gave the stickers to Zeke. He loved them and put them all over his skateboard, which we are ninety-nine percent sure Tanner Gantt stole.

∘ ∘ ∘

They don't sell Randee Rabbit costumes, because no one would buy them, except Zeke. His costume is really an Easter Bunny costume. He adds a red headband, wears a patch on one eye, and puts a little bit of black makeup on his nose. He has a bandolier, which is one of those belts that people wear across their chest with bullets in it, except Zeke puts carrots in his. He looks ridiculous.

When we go trick-or-treating, *nobody* knows

who he's supposed to be. He has to explain it at every single house we go to.

"Trick or treat!"
"Who are you supposed to be, kid?"
"I'm Randee Rabbit!"
"Never heard of him."
"Seriously? You've never heard of Randee Rabbit?!"

Zeke acts like Randee Rabbit is as famous as Harry Potter.

Then Zeke starts to tell them about the game. By that time they usually just give us candy and tell us to go away, so the kids who have started lining up behind us can get their candy. We end up wasting a lot of time and not going to as many houses and not getting as much candy.

I was going to make sure this didn't happen again.

"Zeke, you can't be Randee Rabbit this year."

"I got it covered, Bat-Tom!"

"What do you mean?"

He pulled out a picture of Randee Rabbit. "If people don't know who he is, I'll show them this. On the back it explains about him and the game. I made copies so I can hand them out."

I told Zeke he could be Randee Rabbit at school and the dance, if he wanted to—but I strongly recommended that he didn't, because we were middle-schoolers now. I did tell him he had to wear something different on Halloween night when we went trick-or-treating. If people saw him dressed up as Randee Rabbit, they'd know it was me with him, no matter what costume and mask I was wearing.

I decided to wear the Creepy Clown costume that Mom had found for trick-or-treating. I bet that a lot of kids would be wearing those, but I didn't care. All I cared about was that nobody would know I was a Vam-Wolf-Zom.

32.

Do Not Try on the Masks!

I was in Art class, trying to draw some apples that Mr. Baker had arranged in a bowl, but mine ended up looking like pumpkins. I was also trying to think of a good Halloween school costume that followed the stupid rules, but could maybe win the contest. I looked up at that self-portrait by Vincent van Gogh on the wall and got a great idea.

HALLOWEEN COSTUME PLAN
- Dress up as Vincent Van Gogh for school-day costume contest.

- Impress Art teacher, Mr. Baker, by being his favorite artist, and get a good grade in his class.
- Impress Annie by dressing up as her favorite artist.
- Win Best Costume Contest, because Mr. Baker is one of the judges and so is Mr. Kessler, who wanted to see something "new and different."
- Not look like a Vam-Wolf-Zom at school for once.

o o o

Mom got excited when I told her about my idea that night.

"Van Gogh! I love it! He's my favorite artist."

She had a green coat that looked just like the one in the painting. It was a woman's coat, but I didn't care, it looked perfect. Later that week, she found an old hat in a junk store and dyed it blue. We put a piece of blue fake fur on it, so it looked exactly like Van Gogh's.

I needed to get a pipe and a red beard. I decided to wear a beard, even though he didn't have a beard in the painting, because it would make me look older and more like Van Gogh. This is called artistic license.

Mom made Emma take me to the Halloween store that Saturday. It's a giant store that sells masks and costumes. She wasn't very happy about it.

"Am I Tom's personal chauffeur now?" she moaned. "Why do I have to take him?"

"Because it would be a nice thing to do," said Mom.

"Great!" said Emma. "Should I go around and ask every kid in the neighborhood if they need a ride to the Halloween store?"

"That would be very nice, Emma."

"I was kidding!"

"I know," said Mom, handing her the car keys.

∘ ∘ ∘

Emma complained the whole time she drove me to the store.

"I can't believe I am doing this!"

I decided to change the subject. "What are you going to be for Halloween?"

"Lucas wants us to be a disco couple."

"They'll probably have that at the store."

"Yeah, and it'll probably cost a fortune."

We parked and walked toward the store entrance.

"Okay," said Emma. "You've got *five minutes* to get your junk, then I am leaving."

I could spend a whole day in that store looking at everything, but I was with The Worst Person to Take You to a Halloween Store. They have a million masks and costumes hanging all over the place. We walked in and Emma saw a Cleopatra costume.

"I would look so good in this. And Lucas can be a mummy."

Emma checked out the price.

"Oh my God, this is so expensive!" said The Queen of Complainers.

They make the employees at the Halloween store wear costumes so people will want to buy them. One of the workers, a big guy in a ninja mask and costume, looked up and yelled at us.

"Hey! Can't you read, kid!"

He pointed to a sign behind the counter.

DO NOT TRY ON MASKS!

"Take off that mask right now or you gotta buy it!"

I started to say, "It's not a—"

Emma interrupted me and said, "Shh!"

She turned toward Ninja Guy and gave him one of the most intense glares I've ever seen. It was like she was going to chop his head off. Then, she walked over and got right in his face.

"It's not a mask, you freaking idiot!"

I couldn't believe she yelled at him. Especially about *me*. She never does stuff like that. The guy got flustered.

"Oh. I-I didn't . . . " He looked over at me. "Are you that Vam-Wolf-Zom kid?"

I nodded.

Emma pointed her finger about three inches from his face. "You have just entered a world of trouble!"

"Look, I'm sorry, I didn't—"

"Where's your manager?"

"Please don't call my manager," he begged.

"I am so calling your manager!"

"No, no, no! Please don't!"

Emma put her hands on the glass counter and leaned forward.

"Okay, Mr. Ninja. . . . Are you going to give us a fifty percent discount on what we buy today?"

"What?! I can't do that!"

She turned around and said, "Where is the manager? Can someone get me the manager, right now?"

Ninja Guy freaked out. "Okay, okay! But I can only give you a twenty-five percent discount. That's what they give employees."

Emma's voice got quiet.

"Listen to me . . . carefully. . . . Because I am only going to say this once: You are going to give us a fifty percent discount or I am calling your manager . . . *and* the newspaper . . . *and* the TV news . . . *and* the police . . . and have you arrested for Vam-Wolf-Zom shaming."

Ninja Guy gulped. "Okay. . . . I'll give you fifty percent."

She smiled. "Thank you. Where are your beards and pipes?"

He pointed, and it looked like his hand was shaking. "Aisle two."

We walked down the aisle. You could tell that the other employees were afraid of Emma. They stepped back when we walked by.

"Thanks, Emma," I said.

"What?" she snapped. "I did it for the discount on my Cleopatra costume."

I think she did it for me too. Sometimes Emma is nice. But only about two or three times a year.

A girl in a pirate costume was taking rubber brains out of a box and putting them on a shelf.

"Excuse me?" I asked. "Do you have any red beards?"

She looked up and said, "Arrgh, matey! Are ye going to be a salty old pirate, now? Sure, ye be coming to the proper place then, laddie! Will ye be needing a hook and eye patch and hat and scabbard, me bucko?"

You could tell she liked her job.

"No," I said. "I'm not going to be a pirate. I'm going to be Vincent van Gogh."

Her voice changed to normal. "That is so awesome! I *love* Vincent van Gogh. He is, like, my favorite artist."

He seemed to be a lot of people's favorite artist. Pirate Girl found me a red beard and a plastic pipe.

"You should carry a sunflower too! He *loved* sunflowers."

She found a fake, plastic sunflower for me.

"Okay, come on, let's go," said Emma impatiently.

Mr. Ninja gave us the fifty percent discount. We saved a ton of money.

"Uh, sorry that I thought you had a mask on," he said.

I shrugged. "It's okay."

As we left, Emma glared at him one more time.

33.

Who Are You?

Finally, it was Friday morning, the day before Halloween. I decided to carry a paintbrush and a palette, one of those roundish, flat wooden things artists squeeze paint on. Emma had one when she thought she was an artist for a week and made those pathetic flower paintings.

I put on the jacket, the hat, the beard, and the white bandage over my ear and went down to the kitchen to show Mom and Dad. I couldn't see myself in the mirror, so I had to ask them how it looked.

Dad put down his cup of coffee when I walked in and said, "Don't look now, but Vincent van Gogh has just walked into our kitchen."

"Tommy, you look fantastic!" said Mom.

"Seriously, you've got a shot at winning that contest," said Dad.

I knew Mom and Dad would say something like that, but Emma would tell me if I actually looked good or not. That's one thing she's good at.

"How do I look, Emma?"

She looked at me for two seconds.

"Good."

That's a huge compliment coming from Emma. I decided to add some blood (Emma's red nail polish) to the bandage. There wasn't any blood in Van Gogh's painting, but he did cut himself, so there had to have been *some* blood. And it made the costume feel more like Halloween. And maybe Mr. Baker would think it was more realistic and give me first place in the contest.

o o o

Zeke and I got on the bus in our costumes.

"Looking good, Speedster!" said Bus Lady. She called me Speedster because of the time I ran faster than the bus so I could catch it. "You're that Van Gogh dude."

I always knew she was a smart person.

She looked at Zeke. "Are you The Evil Easter Bunny?"

"No. I'm Randee Rabbit."

"Whatever you say. Take a seat."

We walked down the aisle past kids dressed as Star Wars, Harry Potter, and superhero characters, three pirates, two cheerleaders, and a kid dressed as a piece of bacon. He made me hungry.

Nobody knew who I was dressed as, but I didn't care. I wanted to see what Annie and Mr. Kessler and Mr. Baker, the costume contest judges, would say.

When I saw Annie on the bus, I thought she was dressed up as Abraham Lincoln. She had on a black suit with a long overcoat, a beard, and a black top hat, and for some weird reason she was holding a pole with a little sword on the end. Then I noticed she had a thing on her left leg that make it look like a wooden leg.

"I didn't know Abraham Lincoln had a wooden leg!" said Zeke. "Excellent!"

"He didn't," said Annie. "I'm not Abraham Lincoln. I'm Captain Ahab from *Moby Dick*. He was captain of a whaling ship. This is my harpoon."

Moby Dick was a ginormous book she had read, even though she didn't have to read it for school. I got worried. The judges might like her costume. It looked amazing.

"Tom, your costume is incredible," Annie said.

"Thanks."

"What do you think of my costume, Tom?" asked Capri.

She was dressed like a hippie, with a colorful shirt and fringe vest and jeans. She had daisies in her hair, a headband, and a lot of necklaces. On her vest were buttons that said "Peace" and "Love" and "No Global Warming." The judges might like her costume too, because some of them were old and could have been hippies. She looked like a picture of Gram when she was a teenager.

"Capri, you look like my grandmother," I said.

"What?!"

That didn't go over too well. I tried to tell her it was a compliment, but she didn't believe me. I just meant she looked like a real, authentic hippie.

Zeke said, "I'm Randee Rabbit."

"We know," said Annie and Capri at the same time. They remembered his costume from the year before and the year before that.

That's when Tanner Gantt got on the bus.

The whole bus went dead silent.

For the first time, he was wearing a costume.

34.

Breaking the Rules

Tanner Gantt was wearing a Dino World baseball cap, with a picture of a T. rex playing a guitar on it, that said "Dinosaurs Rock." Just like the one I'd worn the second day of school, after I found out I was Vam-Wolf-Zom. He had white makeup on his face, sunglasses, plastic fangs in his mouth with blood on the tips, a pair of wolf hands with claws, and two furry ears. He was holding a plastic bloody arm, which he was pretending to eat.

Tanner Gantt was dressed up as me.

I have to admit it was an amazing costume. Had he put the whole thing together by himself? How much money had he spent? Or had he gone to the the Halloween store and shoplifted everything?

Some kids on the bus started laughing and looked at me. Tanner Gantt walked down the aisle and smiled.

"Guess who I am?"

"Somebody stupid!" said Zeke.

I couldn't believe Zeke said that. I also couldn't believe that Tanner Gantt didn't punch him.

"You're right, Zimmer-Dork! It *is* somebody stupid, and you're sitting right next to him!" Tanner sat down in the row across from us.

"Not funny!" said Annie from behind me.

"Oh yeah, Barstow? Then why is everybody laughing?"

He had a point. A lot of kids on the bus were laughing.

"Why are you dressed up as Abe Lincoln, Barstow?"

"I'm not talking to you," said Annie.

Tanner Gantt smirked. "You've got a stupid

costume too. But not as stupid as yours, Zimmerman. Why do you wear that same lame bunny outfit every year?"

"He's a rabbit, not a bunny!" said Zeke. "You're going to get in trouble. Principal Gonzales said no vampires or werewolves or zombies!"

Tanner Gantt smiled. "Yeah. I know. But, I'm *not* a vampire or a werewolf or a zombie. I'm a Vam-Wolf-Zom."

Technically, that was true. I was impressed he'd thought of that. But I bet they'd still make him take it off.

"And who are *you* supposed to be, Farts? Some pirate that got shot in the ear?"

"He's Vincent van Gogh," said Capri. "One of the world's greatest artists."

"He looks like The World's Greatest Lame-O."

I didn't care what Tanner Gantt said. I wasn't going to look lame when I won the contest.

○ ○ ○

When we got off the bus at school I saw Abel in his suit and tie, carrying his briefcase, like always.

"Good morning, Mr. Marks. Or should I say, 'Mr. Van Gogh'? Your costume is quite clever. I would venture to say you have a good chance of winning the costume contest."

"Thanks. How come you're not wearing a costume?"

He smiled. "I am." He pulled a pair of dark glasses out of his briefcase and put them on. Then he put an earpiece in his ear, with a curly wire that went into his pocket. "Secret Service agent. Guarding the president."

A bunch of kids were crowded around Dog Hots in front of school. He was dressed up as Frankenstein's monster. It was an incredible costume. His face was greenish gray and he had a realistic-looking scar on his forehead and bolts in his neck. He looked like the monster in the old black-and-white movie that Gram and I have watched a million times.

The makeup was good, but Dog Hots sort of looks like Frankenstein's monster anyway. He's got a big head and a gigantic forehead. And he's tall too. Dog Hots would probably win first place in the contest. But maybe I'd at least get second place or third.

"Awesome Frankenstein costume!" said Zeke.

I corrected him. "He's Frankenstein's *monster*, he's not Frankenstein. That's the name of the doctor. Who did your makeup, Dog Hots?"

"My mom's girlfriend. She's a professional makeup person," said Dog Hots.

Personally, I think that's cheating. I thought about saying something to the judges but decided not to.

○ ○ ○

Principal Gonzales was standing at the front entrance, making sure everybody followed the costume rules. I couldn't wait for him to see Tanner Gantt. It didn't take long.

"Tanner Gantt! Get over here!" said Principal Gonzales, as soon as he saw him. "You can't wear that. No vampire, werewolf, or zombie costumes allowed."

Tanner Gantt looked over at me for a second and grinned. "But, sir, I'm a *Vam-Wolf-Zom*. That's different. The rules don't say we can't dress up as a Vam-Wolf-Zom."

Principal Gonzales shook his head. "You can't wear that, Tanner."

"But I didn't break the rules!"

"You're dressed as a fellow student." He pulled out the rules sheet and read it. "'Costumes may not make fun of any group or individual.'"

I smiled.

Then, Tanner Gantt smiled, which is never a good sign, and pointed at me. "What about Tom? He's breaking the rules."

"How?" said Principal Gonzales.

"He's got excessive blood and he's got a pipe. You can't have pipes at school." He pointed at the rule sheet. "No prohibited substances or paraphernalia." Then he pointed at Annie. "And she's got a weapon."

Principal Gonzales looked over at us. "Annie, Tom, and Tanner come with me."

"It's not a weapon, it's a whaling tool!" said Annie.

"If you're a whale, it's a weapon," said Principal Gonzales.

We followed him to his office. As we passed Dog

Hots, Principal Gonzales said, "Great Frankenstein costume!"

I was going to correct him but decided I probably shouldn't.

35.

Second Offense

anner Gantt, Annie, and I sat in the principal's office. It was my second time there in two months. Annie didn't seem very upset. I couldn't figure out why. There was another kid with a fake knife through his head and one with a bloody chainsaw, and an eighth-grade girl wearing pajamas.

Principal Gonzales pointed at each of us. "Quentin, get rid of the knife in your head. Gunnar, leave the chainsaw here. Sinclair, have a parent bring you other clothes. Tom, take off your bloody bandage and get rid of the pipe. Annie, leave the harpoon in here and pick it up after school. Tanner, take off the furry ears, the fangs, the white makeup, and the hat . . . and leave the arm here."

Everybody started to do as they were told, except for Annie.

"Stop, you guys! We don't have to change," she said.

"Miss Barstow, I don't think you want to push this issue," said Principal Gonzales.

Annie cleared her throat. "Our costumes are protected under the First Amendment to the Constitution of the United States of America. Freedom of speech."

Principal Gonzales sighed. "Annie, the First Amendment does not say you can bring a harpoon to school or have a bloody bandage or dress like a Vam-Wolf-Zom."

"Oh, really?" she said as she pulled out a piece of paper, unfolded it, and started reading out loud. "U.S. Court of Appeals, 1993. A public school is bound by the First Amendment, that promises free expression. Halloween costumes are a form of protected expression. You cannot be investigated or punished for your choice of costume, even if it offends someone else."

I didn't understand everything she said, but it

sounded like we might get to keep our stuff and maybe I could still win the contest, which is all I really cared about.

"All right," said Mr. Gonzales. "You may stay the way you are."

"Yes!" said Annie as she pumped her fist in the air.

"But you have to remain in the detention room today. And you can't be in the contest."

o o o

Everyone did what Principal Gonzales had asked us to do. Except Annie, who wouldn't give up her harpoon. She stormed out all mad and went to the detention room for the whole day.

Without my bloody bandage and pipe I just looked like a guy with a red beard in a green jacket, so I didn't even enter the contest.

Dog Hots got first place for his Frankenstein's monster costume.

A girl named Saria Schnell who dressed as a mouse in a mousetrap (she reminded me of Terrence) got second place.

Zeke won third place for his Randee Rabbit costume. It turned out that Mr. Prady, one of the judges, was a big fan of Rabbit Attack!

Life is completely unfair.

o o o

On the bus ride home from school, I sat with Zeke, who was holding his trophy.

"T-Man, I bet you would've won this if they'd let you wear your whole costume."

I shrugged.

Zeke put his trophy in his backpack.

Annie turned around in the seat in front of us and said, "Do you have another costume for the dance tonight, Tom?"

"Not really. . . . I may not go."

I was feeling sorry for myself, but I sort of liked feeling that way. It's weird how sometimes it feels good to feel bad. Still, you shouldn't feel sorry for yourself for too long because you might miss out on stuff.

"I guess I could wear my old Hermione Granger costume from last year," said Annie.

I remembered that costume. She looked really good in it, except now her hair was short, so she wouldn't look like Hermione. She probably wouldn't buy a wig just for the dance. I would. It bugs me when people don't have the right hair.

"I guess maybe I could find another costume," I said.

Annie got off the bus at her stop. "I hope I see you tonight. Maybe we can dance if the DJ plays a good song."

I couldn't believe it.

Annie Barstow wanted to dance with me tonight.

I had to learn how to dance.

In two and a half hours.

36.

Dance Lesson

When they had dances at my old school, most kids didn't actually dance. They just moved back and forth and waved their arms around. Zeke, of course, went crazy. Sometimes teachers had to ask him to calm down because he got so wild. The two best dancers at our school were Matt Kent and Renee Jaworski, but they were showoffs. I guess if I was that good I would show off too. Tanner Gantt never goes to dances.

I decided to do some research, so I looked at some videos of middle-school dances on YouTube to see what they were like. Groups of girls danced in big circles with one another. Practically all the boys stood in groups, but they didn't dance. Some leaned against a wall and watched. A couple of boys did some break-dance moves. Some boys and girls danced together in groups, and a few actually danced together as couples, but they looked like older kids.

I wanted to ask Mom for a quick dance lesson, but she wasn't home. Emma and Carrot Boy were sitting on the sofa in the living room, pretending to do homework. Emma was the last person in the world I wanted to ask, but like Ben Franklin said, "There are no gains, without pains." And I was desperate.

"Hey, Emma, there's a dance tonight at my school. Can you show me how to not look like an idiot?"

She smiled, sat up, and clapped her hands together.

"Oh, yes! I would love to teach you how to dance! There is nothing in the world I would rather do . . . NOT!"

"Oh, come on, please!"

"I'll teach you how to dance, dude," said Carrot Boy.

Emma freaked. "What? No, will you not."

"C'mon, Emmers, you don't want your brother to be a total doofus out there." He got up off the couch. "I got some sweet moves for you." He played some music on his phone. Then he started dancing.

I had always thought that Zeke was the worst dancer in the world. But Carrot Boy made Zeke look like Matt Kent. I wanted to laugh so bad, but I knew if I did, Emma would kill me. I took a quick glance over at her. I could tell she thought he was pretty bad too.

"Move your arms like this!" he said. "Turn! . . . Spin! . . . Jump! . . . Yeah! . . . Work it, work it!"

Emma quietly went to the window and closed the drapes, so nobody could see in from the outside. Carrot Boy was too into his dancing to notice.

"I made this move up! It's original! Nobody does this!"

Nobody does it, for good reason. He looked ridiculous. He was moving his arms and hands like he was strangling somebody and had to go to the bathroom at the same time.

"I call that The Lucas Lockdown! It is *seriously* hard to do."

He stopped and sat down on the sofa. He was sweaty and out of breath.

"So, dude . . . just do some of those moves . . . and you're good."

"Thanks," I said. "I'll remember everything you did."

I still had to get someone to teach me how to dance and there wasn't much time.

o o o

Since Mom was at the post office mailing packages, I had to ask Dad. I've seen him dance with my mom, and he doesn't look too embarrassing.

"Dad? There's a dance tonight and there's this girl. . . . Can you teach me how to dance in, like, fifteen minutes?"

"Yes sir, I can."

We went up to my room, and I locked the door so Emma wouldn't come in.

"Okay," said Dad seriously. "This may be one of the most important things I ever teach you."

"What do you mean?"

"Ninety percent of guys don't know how to dance and they don't want to know and they never learn. And you know what? They're idiots. Don't be the guy leaning up against the wall, trying to be cool, who never dances. He's missing out. You'll have a lot more fun. You don't have to be great; you just need a few moves. Put on some music."

I played a song and he showed me some simple stuff to do with my feet, and some arm moves. They weren't that hard. And they weren't embarrassing.

"Is there any special girl you want to dance with?" he asked.

"No. . . . Not really. . . . I mean, sort of."

"Does she have a name?"

"Annie Barstow. But don't tell anybody."

He raised his right hand. "My lips are sealed. Ask her to dance. You're only eleven and a half once."

37.

The Witch Surprise

I was going to dress up as a hippie for the dance, because I had all the stuff, but I was worried that Capri would think I was copying her or people would think we were a couple. Then, Carrot Boy said I could borrow his mummy costume. He's short, so it wouldn't be too big on me.

Emma freaked. "Lukey! Don't let Tom wear your costume! You've got to wear it tomorrow night for Pari's Halloween party. Tom'll dance in it and get it all sweaty. Oh my God, it'll smell like stinky Tom!"

"Emmers, chill," said Carrot Boy. "I can wash it if I need to."

Carrot Boy did the makeup on my face and it looked pretty good. I should have been a mummy for the contest. I might have won something. Why does it seem like you always figure out how to do stuff better after it happens?

Dad dropped Zeke (in his award-winning Randee Rabbit costume) and me off at the dance.

"No leaning against the wall," said Dad, when we got out of the car. I nodded.

They had a big sign on the door of the gym:

HALLOWEEN DANCE RULES

- You must present your ticket or buy one when you arrive.

- You must be picked up by an adult at the end of the dance.
- You are not allowed to walk home or ride a bike or scooter or broomstick.
- If you misbehave, your parent/guardian will be called to pick you up early.
- No inappropriate dancing: No moshing, no freaking, no slamming.
- Have fun!

Ms. Heckroth, my super-strict Math teacher, was taking tickets at the door. She was dressed up as a witch and her costume was amazing. She had on a long black dress, a tall witch hat, a black cape, and black leather boots. I never thought in a million years she'd dress up as anything, because she's so serious all the time. It's weird how Halloween gets people to do things you'd never expect.

"Hi, Ms. Heckroth," I said as we gave her our tickets. Zeke was standing behind me. I think he was afraid of her.

"Hello, Mr. Marks, I'm sorry I didn't get to see your Van Gogh costume. I heard it was quite impressive."

"Your costume is impressive," I said. "You make an excellent witch."

I probably shouldn't have said that.

∘ ∘ ∘

They had the lights turned down in the gym, and black and orange balloons everywhere. There were soft drinks and pizza (with no garlic, because of

me). I was glad because even though I'd eaten dinner, I knew I'd get zombie-hungry about halfway through the dance.

The different grades stayed in their own areas, clumped together. Hardly any sixth graders were dancing, except for Matt and Renee, who were showing off in the middle of the gym, like I thought they would.

A bunch of boys were leaning up against the wall, trying to be cool. Coach Tinoco was talking to some of them. He was dressed up as a Roman gladiator.

I think he wore that so he could show off his muscles. I probably would do that too, if I had muscles like him. It was a good costume, but I wished he'd dressed up as The Hulk. He'd look perfect.

I saw the door to the boys' locker room open a crack. Somebody peeked out, and then quickly slipped into the gym. They were wearing a "This Is My Costume" T-shirt. Then I smelled Cheetos.

It was Tanner Gantt, sneaking in without paying.

38.

Dance Police

Why was Tanner Gantt here? I couldn't picture him dancing.

Annie and Capri walked up to us. Capri was in her hippie outfit. Annie was dressed as Hermione and she had a long brown wig on. She looked like the old Annie before she cut her hair over the summer.

"Hey, you bought a wig," I said.

"Yeah. It bugs me when people don't have the right hair for their costume."

Annie was so cool.

"So, do you guys wanna dance?" she asked.

"Excellent!" said Zeke.

"Okay," said Capri. "We'll meet you under the basketball hoop, by the DJ, in five minutes."

They walked off toward the girls' restroom and I turned to Zeke. "Remember, no crazy dancing. Okay?"

He saluted. "Gotcha, VWZ-Man! I gotta go to the bathroom. My mom told me to drink three glasses of water before I got here, so I don't get dehydrated."

He ran off. I headed over toward the basketball hoop and saw Tanner Gantt moshing. He was banging into people, and none of the chaperones noticed. He knocked down a kid dressed up as a French fry, and said, "I'm soooo sorry!" Then he laughed. The kid looked like he was going to cry.

"Hey, you're not supposed to mosh!" I said.

"Why do you care, Freak Boy?" said Tanner Gantt. "Are you the Dance Police?"

"You can't knock people down like that."

He grinned. "Oh, really?" He yelled, "Coach Tinoco!" as he shoved me as hard as he could and then fell on the floor. Coach Tinoco turned just in time to see me bang into Matt and Renee, who both fell down.

"Tom Marks is moshing!" yelled Tanner Gantt, on the floor, pointing at me.

It totally looked like I was moshing.

I tripped over Matt and banged against the DJ's table. His computer slid off the table and the music stopped.

"You broke my computer!" screamed the DJ.

"I'm sorry!" I pointed at Tanner Gantt. "He pushed me!"

Coach Tinoco came running over, like Hulk on a rampage, but dressed like an angry gladiator guy.

"Marks! What do you think you're doing?! No moshing! You are going home!"

I tried to explain. "Tanner Gantt pushed me—"

Coach wouldn't let me finish. "I saw you, Marks!"

"Marks knocked me down!" said Tanner Gantt, who was still on the floor, pretending he was hurt.

"Call someone to come pick you up, Marks," said Coach Tinoco.

o o o

I wanted to turn into a bat and fly home, but I couldn't. I didn't want my parents to know what happened, so I called Emma to come pick me up. She was at a movie with Carrot Boy. She wasn't exactly thrilled.

"Why'd they kick you out?"

"Some kid said I was moshing, but I wasn't!"

"Can't you just walk home?"

"No, Emma. They won't let me."

"You have ruined my life, once again. Be outside when we come! We will wait for five seconds and then we will leave."

o o o

Coach Tinoco walked me outside and made me sit on a bench in the parking lot.

"Stay right here." He jogged back to the gym. He never walks, he always jogs.

I was wondering how mad Emma was going to be. On a scale of 1 to 10, I figured it would be an 8.

"Hey, mummy."

I turned around and saw Annie walking toward me.

"Hey."

She sat down on the bench. "Sorry you got kicked out."

"I wasn't moshing. Tanner Gantt pushed me."

"Yeah, I figured."

We didn't say anything for a while. The music came back on inside the gym. The DJ must have fixed his computer. He was playing a song I had practiced dancing to at home with Dad. It reminded me of summer, before I turned into a Vam-Wolf-Zom and everything changed.

"Let's dance, party people!" yelled the DJ, from inside.

Annie started nodding her head to the beat. "That's a great song."

"Yeah. It is."

"I want to write a song like that, someday."

"I bet you will."

"It's a good song to dance to."

"Yeah. It is."

A couple of more seconds went by. I thought about what my dad said.

"You want to dance?" I asked.

Annie looked at me funny. "Right now?

"Yeah."

"Out here?"

"Yeah."

Annie smiled. "Sure. Why not? We bought tickets. We should at least be able to dance."

I stood up and we started dancing. She was a

good dancer. I remembered most of the moves Dad taught me. We started laughing because it was pretty ridiculous dancing out in the parking lot.

A pickup truck with some teenagers drove by. One of them leaned out the window and yelled, "Hey, Hermione! I'm gonna tell Ron you're dancing with a mummy!"

Annie and I cracked up.

The door to the gym opened and the light shined on us. We stopped dancing. Coach Tinoco came out with Tanner Gantt behind him.

Had Coach Tinoco found out that Tanner Gantt had pushed me into those kids?

"Annie, go back into the gym," said Coach.

She waved to me. "Bye, Tom. Thanks for the dance."

"Can I go back in, Coach?" I asked.

"No, Marks."

Tanner Gantt had gotten in trouble for sneaking into the dance without paying. He couldn't get anyone to pick him up. Coach kept calling and texting his mom, but she didn't answer.

"Is there someone else I can call?" asked Coach. "Another relative? An adult friend?"

"No," he said.

Emma and Carrot Boy drove up in his car. She rolled down her window, gave me a dirty look, and said, "Get in."

"Hey, Coach Tinoco!" said Carrot Boy, leaning across Emma. "Remember me? Lucas Barrington."

"I remember you very well, Barrington."

How could you forget someone who looked like a carrot?

Coach pointed at Tanner Gantt. "We can't reach this boy's parents. Can you take him home?"

"No, Coach, I can walk home," said Tanner Gantt.

"You are *not* walking home," said Coach.

"We can definitely take him home," said Carrot Boy.

I could have killed him.

"Make sure he gets into his house," said Coach. "You're responsible for him, Lucas."

"Gotcha, Coach! No worries. I am on it."

I got in the back seat with Tanner Gantt.

39.

Taco! Taco!

It was weird to be sitting next to Tanner Gantt. We were pretty close to each other because it's a small car and he's big.

"What's your friend's name, Tom?" asked Carrot Boy.

"He's not— His name's Tanner Gantt."

"Hey, Tanner. I'm Lucas."

Tanner Gantt didn't say anything.

"Where do you live, Tanner?" asked Emma impatiently.

"Three-five-zero-zero North Isabel," he mumbled. "By the park."

Emma put the address in her phone to find it. "Let's go, Lukey."

"Seat belts on, dudes," he said. "Prepare for hyperspace."

We drove out of the parking lot at, like, five miles an hour.

Carrot Boy looked at me in the rearview mirror.

"So, Tom? Did you use any of the sweet dance moves I showed you, before they kicked you out?"

"Uh . . . a few," I lied.

"You didn't try the Lucas Lockdown, did you?"

"No way." That was the truth.

All of a sudden, I got zombie-hungry. I hadn't had a chance to get pizza at the dance. "Emma, I need to get some food."

"We are so *not* stopping for food," she said.

"I'm kinda hungry too," said Carrot Boy.

"I am not hungry at all," said Emma.

I pointed my arm in between their seats.

"Look, there's a Taco! Taco! in the next block."

"I *love* Taco! Taco!" said Carrot Boy.

"I *hate* Taco! Taco!" said Emma. "Can't you wait, Tom?"

"No, I gotta eat something right now."

Tanner Gantt looked worried. I think he thought I was going to eat him.

"We'll be home in ten minutes!" said Emma.

"I'm *really* hungry, Emma."

Tanner Gantt moved as far away from me as he could, leaning against the door.

o o o

We went to the Taco! Taco! drive-through and ate in the car. I got three carne asada tacos. Carrot Boy got a burrito, which Emma fed to him as he drove. That was kind of gross. Emma got nachos, even though she "wasn't hungry at all." Tanner Gantt didn't get anything, even when Carrot Boy offered to pay. He just stared out the window.

When we pulled up in front of his house, the lights were on and loud music was blaring from inside. There were a lot of cars and some motorcycles parked on the street.

"Looks like it's party time at Gantt Manor," said Carrot Boy.

That was weird. Coach had called his mom a million times and nobody answered. Tanner Gantt got out of the car.

"Later, Tanner Dude," said Carrot Boy.

We watched him walk up to the house.

"Oh my God! He didn't even say 'thank you.'" Emma leaned her head out the window and yelled, "You're welcome!"

Tanner Gantt didn't say anything or turn

around. He knocked on his front door. Why didn't he have a key?

"Let's go, Lukey," said Emma.

Tanner Gantt turned around to look at us. You could tell he wanted us to leave.

"We can go," I said from the back seat.

"No, we gotta make sure he gets inside," said Carrot Boy. "I don't want Coach Tinoco going all Roman gladiator on me."

Tanner Gantt kept knocking on the door. He turned around to look at us again.

"You can go!" he yelled.

"Not till you get in, dude!" Carrot Boy yelled back.

The door finally opened and his mom was standing there. She has long blond hair and wears a lot of makeup and dresses like she's in high school. I could hear them talking because of my Vam-Wolf-Zom ears.

"What are you doing here?" she said. She didn't sound happy.

"The dance ended early," he mumbled.

"Why?"

"I dunno."

"Did you get in trouble? What'd you do this time?"

"I didn't do anything! Let me in."

She looked over his shoulder at Carrot Boy's car. "Who brought you home?"

"A kid from school called his sister."

"Well, go spend the night at your friend's house."

"He's not my friend."

She came out of the house and dragged him with her, down to the car. She was smiling and talked in a fake nice voice.

"Hey, guys! What's up? I'm Tanner's mom. But y'all can call me Brandi."

"Hi. I'm Lucas, this is Emma, and her brother, Tom."

"Awesome! Great to meet you! Tanner never brings any of his friends over. Hey, Tom, can Tanner spend the night at your house?"

That was The Worst Idea in the History of the World.

"Sorry, Brandi," said Emma, using *her* fake nice voice. "He can't tonight. My mother's sick. She has this really contagious, infectious disease."

For once I was glad that Emma was The Queen of Liars.

"She does?" asked Carrot Boy.

Mrs. Gantt looked at me in the back seat. "Did Tanner get in trouble at the dance?"

I should have said yes, but for some reason I

said no. I think I just wanted to get out of there.

Mrs. Gantt's eyes got super wide.

"Oh my God! You're the Vam-Wolf-Zom kid! Tanner, why didn't you tell me he was your friend?" She leaned into my window. "I am so sorry; I didn't recognize you. I saw you on TV. You are such a brave little guy! Can you turn into a bat and fly?"

"No, ma'am, I can't," I said.

"And polite too!" She shoved Tanner Gantt in the shoulder. "Why aren't you polite like that?" She turned back at me. "Hey, I got a great idea! You guys all want to come in to the party? There are some friends of mine who would *love* to meet you."

I knew she just wanted to show me off to her friends.

"Sorry, Brandi," said Emma. "We just picked up some special pills for my mother and if she doesn't take them in, like, fifteen minutes, she'll die. Bye! Let's go, Lukey!"

As we drove away, I looked out the back window. Mrs. Gantt yelled at Tanner Gantt and then she went back in the house. He walked across the street to the park and sat down on the swings. I felt a little bit sorry for him. But not too sorry.

40.

All Hallow's Eve

On Halloween night, even though I had told Zeke a million times he couldn't wear it, he showed up in his Randee Rabbit costume.

Sort of.

He had put a hockey mask on over the rabbit head and he was carrying a plastic bloody machete in one hand and an Easter basket with a chopped-off head in the other. I have to admit, it looked pretty good.

"See, T-Man, I'm *not* Randee Rabbit! I'm the Evil Easter Bunny, like Bus Lady said."

He held up the bloody machete and made a noise that was supposed to be an evil rabbit growling. It sounded like he was gargling. He should go on YouTube and find a video that teaches you how to do sound effects.

"Zeke, it's still too close to Randee Rabbit. People will know it's you and so they'll know it's me with you. This is the only night of the whole year that I don't have to be a Vam-Wolf-Zom."

I made him wear an old skull mask and black hood I had. He was disappointed at first, but got over it and started making what he called "Mr. Skull Man Noises." It sounded like he was yodeling.

I put on the Creepy Clown costume. The box said "Medium," but it was a "Small." It was super tight on me and the arms and legs were too short, but I didn't have anything else to wear.

○ ○ ○

We started trick-or-treating as soon as it got dark. It seemed like a lot of people were dressed up as vampires and werewolves and zombies this year. Or maybe I noticed it more because I was a Vam-Wolf-Zom.

We passed a tall girl dressed as a nurse covered in blood. I got a little thirsty. Luckily, Mom had some raw liver in the fridge for when I got home.

Down the block, we saw Dog Hots and Elliot
Freidman, from Art class. I wanted to see if they'd
recognize me. I made Zeke hide behind a bush, so
he wouldn't accidentally say something.

I walked up to them.

"Hey, you guys," I said, making my voice sound
higher.

Dog Hots laughed. "You got a funny voice, kid."

"Uh, yeah, I got a cold."

"And you got the wrong-sized costume on too."

"I know. My mom put it in the dryer and
it shrunk. That's an awesome Frankenstein
costume."

I didn't say "Frankenstein's monster," because nobody ever does and Dog Hots might know it was me.

"Hey, does that Vam-Wolf-Zom kid live around here?" I asked.

"Tom Marks?" said Elliot. "Yeah, he does."

Elliot was dressed as the Where's Waldo guy, which was a good costume for him because he could wear his glasses.

"Do you know him?" I asked.

"Yeah. We go to school with him," said Elliot. "He drew my picture in Art class."

"What's he like?"

Dog Hots shrugged. "He's okay, I guess."

Okay? That was it? I was just "okay"?

"I heard he can do cool stuff," I said. "Like, he's really strong and fast and has super hearing and night vision."

"Yeah, but he can't turn into a bat and fly," said Dog Hots.

Why did *EVERYONE* want me to turn into a bat and fly?!

"C'mon, let's go," said Elliot, and they walked away.

They didn't know who I was.

This was going to work!

41.

Dumbness

Zeke and I got a lot of candy, but some people gave out weird stuff.

WEIRD STUFF THAT PEOPLE GAVE OUT ON HALLOWEEN

1. Breath mints: I told the people that technically those weren't candy. They said, "Take it or leave it, kid." I took it. I'll give it to Emma.

2. A comic book called "The Real Truth About Halloween!": It was pretty boring except for the cover, which had a devil eating two kids dressed as ghosts.

3. A bag of Cheetos: Tanner Gantt would love that house, if he went trick-or-treating.

4. Hot Sauce Packets from Taco! Taco!: They had run out of candy and felt like they had to give us something. Zeke ate his and coughed for about five minutes.

5. A toothbrush: The people giving those out thought it was hilarious. I didn't.

o o o

We'd just left a house that gave us black licorice (yuck) when two high-schoolers came up to us. One was dressed as Wonder Woman, although she had *blond* hair, when she should have *black* hair. The other was Groot, the talking tree, from *Guardians of the Galaxy*.

"Does that Vam-Wolf-Zom kid live around here?" asked Wonder Woman.

"Yeah!" said Zeke. "And he's really awesome. He's like the coolest person I know."

"Are you the president of his fan club?" said Wonder Woman, and then she laughed like it was the world's greatest joke.

Zeke's eyes lit up. "No, I'm not. . . . But he *should* have a fan club! Excellent idea!"

"We want to get a selfie with him," said Groot.

"You can't do that," I said.

"Why? Is he stuck-up or something?"

"No," I said. "He doesn't show up in pictures because he's a vampire."

"Can he turn into a bat and fly?" asked Groot.

"No," I said for the millionth time.

Groot laughed. "That's dumb."

"Yeah?" I said. "Well, you know what else is dumb? When you dress up as Groot you're only supposed to say, 'I am Groot.'"

"Oh yeah?" said Wonder Woman. "What's *really* dumb is when you wear a clown costume that's two sizes too small!"

"You know what's even dumber than that?" I said. "A Wonder Woman with blond hair!"

She called me a lot of nasty words as they walked off.

○ ○ ○

Since Zeke didn't have to explain to everybody who Randee Rabbit was, we went to so many more houses and got our best candy haul ever. Our pillowcases were practically full. We took a shortcut back to my house, but we shouldn't have. Just like Martha Livingston shouldn't have taken that shortcut through that dark alley.

42.

The Shortcut

We were on a block we don't usually go to. There weren't any kids trick-or-treating because most of the houses didn't have their lights on. That means the people who live there ran out of candy or they hate Halloween and don't want kids banging on their door.

There was a big teenager, in a greasy T-shirt, working on a motorcycle in a driveway. An even bigger teenager came out of the garage, flipping a wrench up and down in his hand, as we walked by.

"Hey, Skull Face," said Big Teenager. "Cool costume."

"Thanks," said Zeke.

"Come here, kid. I wanna check it out."

"Don't, Zeke," I whispered.

It was too late. Zeke was walking up the driveway. They didn't look like the kind of teenagers interested in some kid's costume.

"You got a lot of candy," said Big Teenager.

"We did!" said Zeke. "Twice as much as last year."

"That's cool. Hey, we didn't have time to go trick-or-treating, can we have a piece?"

"Sure," said Zeke, opening his bag.

I knew he'd do that because he's generous. And he trusts everybody. I have to remind him not to do that.

Zeke looked down in his bag.

"What would you like? I got Butterfinger, Snickers, Twix, um, breath mints, Kit Kat, Nerds, Sour Patch . . . licorice . . . Skittles."

"Gee, I can't decide," said Big Teenager. "I guess I'll have to take the whole bag."

He grabbed Zeke's bag and laughed.

"Hey! What are you doing?" said Zeke.

Bigger Teenager turned to me.

"Give me your bag, Clown Boy."

We had walked a long way and worked hard to get all that candy. I was not going to give it to these guys.

"No," I said.

Bigger Teenager started walking toward me. Now, if I wasn't a Vam-Wolf-Zom I would have given it to him. Since I can run super fast, I knew I could get away from these guys, but I also knew Zeke couldn't.

Bigger Teenager tried to grab my bag. I pulled it away and put it behind my back. He looked surprised at how fast I moved.

"Give me the bag, kid!"

"No. And give my friend back his candy," I said.

Bigger Teenager laughed. "Who's gonna make me?"

Zeke said, "You don't wanna mess with him, you guys."

"We don't?" said Big Teenager. "Why not, Clown Boy?"

"Because he's a—"

"Shh," I said to Zeke.

I moved over to the motorcycle and lifted it off the ground with one hand. The teenagers seemed surprised that a kid in a too-small clown costume could do that.

"What the—?!" said Big Teenager.

"Put it down, kid!" said Bigger Teenager.

The motorcycle felt like it weighed nothing. I could have held it up all night.

"Okay," I said. "Here's what we're going to do. . . . You're going to give my friend back his bag of candy. Then we're going to leave. If you don't give his bag back, by the count of three, I'm going to throw your motorcycle into the street. One . . ."

"Don't!" said Bigger Teenager.

"Two . . ."

I raised the motorcycle up over my head.

"Holy—!"

Big Teenager tossed the bag at Zeke. Some of the candy spilled out.

"Pick it up," I said.

Both of the teenagers picked up the candy, put it in the bag, and gave it to Zeke. I still wanted to throw the motorcycle in the street, but they'd probably sue me and I'd have to buy a new one, so I put it down.

Bigger Teenager said, "Who are you?"

"Me? I'm just a clown."

∘ ∘ ∘

Zeke wanted to go to one more house, the one with a monster maze in the backyard. But it's just little kids in masks jumping out at you in the dark and screaming. And with my night vision I'd be able to see where they were hiding.

So, I left him there and started walking home by myself. I was going to have some candy, a little raw liver, and watch an old, scary movie that Gram recommended called *Carnival of Souls*.

I was walking toward the park. It was empty, because they close it off on Halloween night so people don't go in and wreck stuff. On the corner, I saw Tanner Gantt in his "This Is My Costume" T-shirt, talking to a girl dressed up as a vampire. He was laughing and smiling, which he usually doesn't do unless he's just thrown you in a trash can. I figured he was going to take her candy, but she didn't have a bag.

I didn't want to deal with Tanner Gantt tonight. As I turned around to go the other way, I heard the girl laugh.

I stopped.

It couldn't be.

I turned around.

The girl Tanner Gantt was talking to had long red hair and pale white skin and was wearing a dark green dress.

It was Martha Livingston.

43.

Saving Tanner Gantt

*H*ow did Martha Livingston get here?

    What was she doing here?

Why was she talking to Tanner Gantt?

I slipped behind a tree, peeked out, and cocked my ear toward them to listen.

"That's an awesome T-shirt!" said Martha.

She wasn't talking in her normal voice. She sounded like one of those teenage girls who get excited about everything.

"Thanks," said Tanner.

Martha smiled.

"Whoa!" he said. "Those fangs look real."

"You think so?"

"Yeah. I wouldn't want you to bite me."

Martha laughed, like it was the funniest joke anyone had ever told.

"My name's Martha, what's yours?"

"Tanner."

"That's a cool name."

I have to admit, Tanner *is* a cool name.

"Hey, do you know that Vam-Wolf-Zom kid?" asked Martha, twirling the end of her hair with her finger.

"Tom Marks? Yeah. He goes to my school."

"Really? He does?" said Martha, pretending to be impressed. "Where does he live?"

"A couple of blocks away."

"What's he like?"'

I figured he'd say something like, "He's a total dork. He's so stupid that he got bit by a vampire and a werewolf and a zombie on the same freaking day. And he's a vampire, but he can't even turn into a bat and fly! What a loser!"

But this is what he said to Martha: "Tom's cool. We hang out all the time. We're like best friends. I'm in a band with him."

Why was Tanner Gantt saying that?

"Awesome!" said Martha, in her goofy-teenager

voice. "Hey, Tanner, I heard some kids say there's a scary monster maze on the other side of the park. You want to check it out with me?"

"Sure."

"Awesome!" said Martha. "Let's go through the park."

"We can't. It's closed on Halloween."

"So? Are you . . . *afraid* to go that way?"

"No!"

"Then let's go!"

o o o

Martha was going to take Tanner Gantt in the park and suck his blood. She might accidentally turn him. We did not need a vampire Tanner Gantt. I had to stop her. I had to get him out of there, even though he wouldn't do it for me.

I pulled my creepy clown mask down over my face and ran out from behind the tree. I hoped Tanner wouldn't recognize me. Would Martha?

"Hey! Are you Tanner Gantt?" I said in my high-pitched voice.

"Yeah. Who are you? Minnie Mouse?"

"Uh, no. My name's . . . Lucas."

I glanced over at Martha. It didn't look like she knew it was me.

He smirked. "I think you bought the wrong-sized costume, dork."

I looked down at my tight costume. "It shrunk. Listen, your mom's looking for you, she said you had to come home right now!"

"Why?"

"She said it was an emergency!"

"What happened?"

"Your . . . your dog got hit by a car!"

Tanner Gantt had a dog that was big and mean, just like him.

He looked worried. "Is he okay?"

"I don't know! You better go see!"

He turned to Martha. "I gotta go. Maybe I'll see you later."

She smiled. "I hope so."

Tanner Gantt ran off down the sidewalk.

Martha slowly turned to me and smiled.

"So . . . Lucas? Do you want to go see a scary monster maze?"

I couldn't believe it. Martha didn't know it was me.

"No. . . . I already went."

She moved closer and started whispering. "Come on, Lucas. . . . We can cut through the park. . . . You want to go in the park with me . . . don't you?"

She was trying to hypnotize me.

"No, I don't, Martha!"

I pulled off my mask.

She put her hand to her mouth and let out a little gasp. "Thomas Marks. . . . What a pleasant surprise."

"What are you doing here?!"

"I am en route to New Orleans. You were on the way, so, I thought I'd drop by to see how you were faring."

"Were you going to suck Tanner Gantt's blood?"

"That was the general idea, before I was rudely interrupted."

I looked around to make sure no one was watching us. I didn't really need to worry. We just looked like a girl dressed up as a vampire and a kid in a clown costume talking to each other on Halloween.

"I must feed," she said.

"Let's go to my house," I said. "I have some raw liver you can have."

She made a disgusted face. "*Raw liver?* I suppose that will have to do, until I can find a *real* meal."

"Just don't bite anybody here. Blood swear."

She sighed. "Blood swear."

We started walking down the sidewalk, through groups of trick-or-treaters.

"How'd you find out where I live?" I asked.

"Quite simple. I used the magic power of . . . Google."

We passed two parents pushing a stroller with a baby in it who was dressed as a vampire.

"Are there any baby vampires?" I whispered to Martha as we passed.

"I've only met one," she said. "Extremely difficult to babysit."

"Okay, listen, when we get to my house, I'll go in first. You wait outside, turn into a bat, fly up to my window, and I'll let you in. Make sure you find a dark place to transform, so no one sees you."

"Must I remind you, Thomas Marks, that I have been doing this for over two hundred years?"

As we turned the corner to my house, we practically bumped into Annie and Capri.

44.

Are Those Real?

Hey, Tom," said Annie.

Why hadn't I pulled my creepy clown mask back over my face?

Annie was wearing her Captain Ahab *Moby Dick* outfit and carrying her harpoon. Capri was in her hippie outfit.

"Hey, you guys," I said.

"Is your costume, like, two sizes too small?" asked Capri.

"It shrunk. Did you get a lot of candy?"

"Yeah," said Annie, looking at Martha. Capri was looking at her too.

I was trying to think of what to say, when Martha put out her hand.

"Good evening. I am Martha Livingston of Philadelphia."

Annie and Capri looked at each other. Maybe they thought Martha was talking weird because she was pretending to be a vampire. Kids don't usually shake hands either. Except Abel, of course. Annie shook Martha's hand.

"Whoa. Your hand is cold," said Annie.

"I have . . . poor blood circulation," said Martha.

"I'm Annie."

"I'm Capri."

Martha shook Capri's hand and then turned back to Annie.

"I must say, that is an excellent Captain Ahab costume."

I think Annie was surprised that Martha knew who Captain Ahab was. "Thanks. You've read *Moby Dick*?"

"Twice," said Martha, then she turned to Capri. "And your costume is quite well done. Except for the 'No Global Warming' button, which is historically inaccurate for the sixties."

"I don't care," said Capri.

"Obviously," said Martha.

Annie looked at Martha's outfit. "So, what are *you* supposed to be?"

Martha smiled and showed her fangs. "Guess?"

"A vampire," said Annie.

"Correct."

"Where'd you get your fangs?" asked Capri.

"It's a long story."

"Is that a wig?" asked Annie.

"No," said Martha as she moved her head so her hair swirled around. "This is my hair."

"Those contact lenses make your eyes look super-intense green," said Capri.

"I'm not wearing contact lenses," said Martha.

Annie got a strange expression on her face and looked at me.

"Wait. . . . Isn't Martha Livingston the name of the girl who wrote the diary about Ben Franklin?"

Why did Annie have to have such a good memory?

"Uh . . . yeah," I said. "Did you guys go to the house where they gave out hot sauce?"

Annie turned to Martha. "And *your* name is Martha Livingston and you're from Philadelphia."

I quickly added, "She's her great-great-great-great-great-great-granddaughter."

I hoped I'd used enough "greats."

Annie went on. "And you're thirteen and you play a lot of musical instruments."

"Eleven, to be precise," said Martha. "My goodness. It appears that Thomas has told you a great deal about me."

"*Thomas*?" said Annie. "You call him Thomas?"

"That is his name, I believe?" said Martha.

I had to get us out of there. I tugged on the collar of my costume. "This costume is cutting off my blood circulation, I gotta take it off. I'll see you at school on Monday."

"So, what are you doing here, Martha?" said Capri.

"Trick-or-treating, of course."

"So, where's your candy bag?" said Annie.

"I left it at Thomas's house."

"Yeah, and we better get back there," I said. "Your parents are going to pick you up and take you to New Orleans, where you're going to live forever. Bye, Annie, Capri. See you at school!"

"Bye, Martha," said Capri. "Really nice to meet you. Sorry we can't hang out." You could tell she was being sarcastic.

"Bye, *Thomas*," said Annie.

They walked off, whispering to each other. But I didn't listen because I was explaining to Martha about the diary I made up in class for my report and promised I hadn't told anybody about her.

Martha watched them go and said, "Annie is quite fond of you."

"What— What are you talking about?"

"As is Capri."

"No, she isn't! "

Martha grinned.

"So? Have you flown outside yet, Thomas?"

I knew she was going to ask that.

"Um . . . not really. . . . I'm still working on my landings. But I'm going to do it soon."

"Why not tonight?"

"Tomorrow's better. I'll definitely do it tomorrow."

"My dear Thomas Marks, pile up enough tomorrows and you'll find you've collected nothing but a lot of empty yesterdays."

"Did Ben Franklin say that?"

Before she could answer, I saw Zeke running down the sidewalk toward us.

"T-Man!"

45.

Hypnotic Lesson

Why was *everybody* I know showing up?

Zeke ran up and said, "Somebody told Tanner Gantt his dog got run over! But it didn't! And he was—"

He saw Martha and he froze. His jaw dropped and he slowly raised his hand and pointed at her.

"You're . . . you're her. . . . The girl . . . the bat . . . that bit Tom. . . . The vampire. . . . You're Martha Livingston!"

Martha glared at me. Her glares were scarier than Emma's.

"You told this lad about me?!"

"No! I-I didn't. He guessed! And I didn't melt or burn up, so I didn't break the blood oath." I jumped in between Zeke and Martha. "Swear on blood you won't bite him!"

"I swear on blood," she said, through gritted teeth. She curtsied to Zeke and said, "Martha Livingston of Philadelphia."

Zeke put his hand over his heart and bowed, like she was a queen or something.

"Zeke Zimmerman at your service, m'lady."

"Pleased to make your acquaintance." Martha turned to me. "A lad with manners. How refreshing. So, this is your true and loyal friend."

"You're even prettier than T-Man said you were!"

Why do I tell Zeke *anything*?

He raised his hand. "I solemnly promise I will never tell anybody about you, Martha!"

She moved closer to Zeke and softly said, "I know you won't, Zeke."

"Your eyes are super green," he said.

She kept staring at him as she spoke. "You won't tell anyone about me. Because . . . I was never here. . . . You never saw me."

"I . . . never . . . saw . . . you," said Zeke in a sleepy voice.

"You hypnotized him that fast?" I said.

She nodded. "He is the most willing subject I have yet encountered. Is there anything you wish him to do while under the trance?"

I thought about that for a while. "Can you ask him to stop doing jumping jacks when he gets excited?"

"As you wish," she said, turning to Zeke. "The next time you want to do jumping jacks, Zeke, you will refrain from doing so. . . . You will not do them, ever again. . . . And now, you will go home and have a restful slumber."

Zeke walked down the sidewalk in a daze, repeating, "No . . . more . . . jumping jacks. . . . No . . . more . . . jumping jacks."

"Martha? Can you teach me how to hypnotize people?" I asked.

"I can try."

o o o

She turned into a bat in my backyard. I went in the house, told Mom and Dad how trick-or-treating went, grabbed the liver from the fridge, went up to my room, locked the door, took off my creepy clown outfit, opened my window, and let Martha in.

I sat on the bed, she sat at my desk, and we split the raw liver.

"This is . . . *horrid*," she said after one bite and put the plate down. "Let us commence with the hypnosis lesson." She stood up. "You cannot make someone fall in love with you. You cannot make someone hurt themselves. And some people will never bend to your will."

I knew what she meant. I had tried to hypnotize Tanner Gantt the first week of school, so he'd stop bothering me. He *pretended* to be hypnotized and then he threw me into a trash can. If someone doesn't want to be hypnotized they can't be, which is unfair. It's like having a superpower you can't use.

"Rise and face me," said Martha.

I stood up and we looked at each other.

"Lock eyes with the subject. Stare intently. You may simply think of what you want them to do, but usually you must speak it aloud."

"Okay."

"It does help to get as close as possible to your subject, as you witnessed when I hypnotized Zeke."

I took a step toward her.

"Look into my eyes," she whispered.

Her eyes really were super green. She also had some freckles on her nose that you can't see unless you're up close.

"You must talk quietly . . . calmly . . . slowly. . . . Do not let them look away."

Her voice was relaxing. I felt a little sleepy.

"Thomas?"

"Yes?"

"Do you have a diary?"

"Yes."

"Go get your diary and let me read it."

I got down on the floor and reached way under my bed. I pulled out my old baseball glove. Inside was a black notebook. I handed it to Martha, and she started reading it out loud.

"'Tuesday. December 25. If you are not named Thomas Marks, do not read this diary or you will be killed! If you are Emma, I will tell Mom and Dad I saw you smoking a cigarette with Pari in her car.

"'Emma got me this diary for Christmas. It's a really cheap one. I think she got it at the one-dollar store. I'm going to write in this every single day.

"'Christmas was pretty good. I got a lot of cool stuff, except for this diary. Zeke called me to say he got a new video game called Rabbit Attack! He said it was the greatest game ever, so I'm going to buy it.'"

Martha turned the page.

"It's blank?"

She turned more pages. They were blank too.

"You only wrote in your diary *once*?"

"Yes."

She snapped her fingers. I felt like I woke up from a nap. She tossed the diary on my bed.

"Hey! Did you just read my diary?" I asked, annoyed.

"All *one* page of it? Yes. Now, be properly warned, Thomas Marks: The power to hypnotize is a dangerous one. What you make someone do may come back to haunt you . . . in unpleasant ways."

"Okay," I said. "Can you teach me how to turn into mist or fog?"

"Not in one night. That is the most difficult transformation to perform. It requires immense skill. However, I have something for you."

She reached into a pocket in her dress and pulled out a small book, with a worn and cracked leather cover.

"I learned much from this," she said, handing it to me.

On the cover, in faded, gold letters, it said "*A Vampiric Education* written by Eustace Tibbitt. "

"This was a gift from my instructor, Lovick Zabrecky. Only one hundred copies were printed. If it fell into other hands . . . I would be greatly displeased. It is quite valuable. Do *not* sell it on eBay."

"Thanks."

I flipped through it. The pages were thin and yellowed. There were some drawings of people in Ben Franklin–type clothes, turning into mist and smoke and fog and bats and wolves. I put it in my baseball glove, along with my diary, and hid it back under the bed.

"What happened to that guy, Lovick Zabrecky?" I asked.

"I have neither seen nor heard from him for over a hundred years. I suppose he was staked or perished in the sun. Would you like me to demonstrate a transformation to smoke, before I take my leave?"

"Yeah!"

She closed her eyes. Then she was gone, and there was a small white cloud about Martha's size. It moved across the room, went under the crack in the door and disappeared.

"FIRE!" screamed Emma in the hallway.

I quickly unlocked my door and opened it. Emma was standing there, dressed in her Cleopatra costume, freaking out and pointing at the fog.

"Fire! Fire!"

"No, Emma! It's not!" I yelled. "Shh! It's not a fire!"

"What is it?" she said, holding her nose.

"It's . . . uh . . . it's a smoke-bomb magic trick that somebody gave us for trick-or-treat."

Smoky Martha went back through the door and into my bedroom.

"I never got anything that good on Halloween!" said Emma. She went into her room and slammed the door.

"Don't slam doors!" yelled Dad from some-where.

I went back in my room and closed the door. The smoke was over by the window and turned back into Martha.

"Your sister is as spirited as ever."

"Yeah. She is. That smoke thing is pretty amazing."

"It is an excellent way to get in and out of places surreptitiously. Now, I must depart."

"Why are you going to New Orleans?" I asked.

"For The Gathering, of course," she said, like I was supposed to know.

"Of vampires?"

She rolled her eyes. "No, bagpipe players. Of course vampires!"

"Is it, like, a vampire convention? Like a Vampire-Con?" That sounded cool.

"No!" she sneered. "We do not trade Dracula action figures, or have costume contests or vampire sing-alongs, or buy and sell capes, or watch vampire movie marathons. . . . It is a serious event. Especially as our numbers dwindle. It is about survival and existing in the modern world."

That sounded kind of boring.

Martha tilted her head slightly and narrowed her eyes. "However . . . *you* would be quite the sensation, if you were to attend. Many would be curious to meet you—the world's one and only Vam-Wolf-Zom. Perhaps you would care to join me?"

I didn't want to hang out with a bunch of vampires staring at me.

"No, thanks."

"Perhaps another time. Farewell, Thomas Marks."

"Bye, Martha."

"Good luck with your lessons, vampiric and scholastic . . . and with Annie and Capri," she added with a smile.

She turned into a bat, hovered at the windowsill, and flew out into the night past the half moon. She made flying look so easy, but she'd been doing it for two hundred and forty-four years.

I was hungry. But not for blood or meat. I made some popcorn and settled down in the den with my pillowcase of candy. I turned off all the lights—which is what you should do when you watch a scary movie—and put on *Carnival of Souls*. Emma and Carrot Boy came home just as it started.

"Is this one of Gram's boring, old black-and-white movies?" said Emma.

I ignored her.

"This looks awesome!" said Carrot Boy, plopping down on the sofa.

Emma had a semi-meltdown. "Lukey, we're not going to watch this!"

"C'mon, Emmers, it's Halloween; we gotta watch a scary movie."

She sat down and ate three of my best candy bars. She kept saying the movie wasn't scary, but she hid her face behind a pillow about ten times.

When it ended, Carrot Boy said to me, "Dude, we should start a Scary Movie Club!"

"No we shouldn't!" said Emma.

All in all it wasn't a bad first Halloween as a Vam-Wolf-Zom.

46.

Down the Rabbit Hole

I woke up the next morning and Emma was in my
room. She was standing by my desk, reading a
letter.

I sat up in bed. "What are you doing?!"

"Reading a letter from your girlfriend."

"WHAT?!"

I jumped out of bed.

"Give it to me! Why are you reading it?"

"I thought it was to me," said Emma. "There
was no name on it."

"Emma! It was a letter on *my* desk, in *my* room, and you thought it was for you?!"

I tried to grab it, but I didn't want to tear it, in case it was important. Emma read it out loud.

"'Dearest Thomas Marks . . .'"

Emma looked up. "That's a little formal, don't you think?"

Martha must have come back and left the letter after I was asleep. Why?

"'We, who are not like others, must traverse a road that is not easily traveled. I wish you luck in your life. I am glad I was able to teach you a few things.'"

She looked up again. "Oooo! What did she teach you?"

I ignored her. She kept reading.

"'But take heed, you must spread your wings and fly in the world. As Benjamin Franklin said, '*Nothing ventured, nothing gained.*'"

Emma made a face. "Seriously? She's quoting Ben Franklin? Who is this girl?"

"'Fondly yours, Martha Livingston.'"

Emma shook her head. *"Fondly* is not good."

"'P.S. Do not forget to floss.'"

"Are you kidding me? Who says 'floss' at the end of a love letter? Does your girlfriend want to be a dentist when she grows up?"

"She's not my girlfriend!"

"How old is she?

"Thirteen."

"Ooo! An older woman! Who is she?"

"None of your business!"

Emma dropped the letter on my desk and walked out the door and down the hall. "Tom has a new girlfriend named Martha Livingston!"

"Who's Martha Livingston?" yelled Mom from the living room.

"What happened to Annie Barstow?" yelled Dad from the living room.

∘ ∘ ∘

Later that day I went over to Zeke's to see if Martha's hypnotizing had really worked on him. He didn't say anything about seeing her, but I had to try one more thing.

"Hey, Zeke, do you want to play Rabbit Attack!?"

I *never* ask Zeke to play Rabbit Attack! He knows how much I hate it.

"Really, T-Man? Excellent!"

Normally, he would have started doing jumping jacks. But he didn't.

Martha had cured him.

We started playing and it was just as boring as I remembered.

"T-Man, want to see a really cool thing?"

I pretended I was interested. "Sure, Zeke."

"See that little rabbit hole in the corner of the screen? Throw three carrots down there."

I threw three carrots down the hole, and Randee Rabbit went to this amazing underworld. There were cool weapons and big battles and robot rabbits and awesome creatures. We played for

three hours until my mom said I had to come home. Rabbit Attack! is the greatest game ever.

"Zeke, why didn't you tell me how cool this game was?" I said as I was leaving.

"I did. About a million times.

But you never listened. You only played it that one time."

"Sorry, Zeke."

"It's cool, T-Man."

Sometimes Zeke is right about stuff. I have to remember that.

o o o

That night, I thought about what Martha had said about "spreading my wings and flying in the world."

I decided I was going to try flying outside. I was ready to do it, but then I looked up "owls and bats" on YouTube. I watched some videos of owls chasing bats. They end up catching them and eating them. I strongly suggest you don't watch them. They are terrifying and gross.

I decided to wait a little longer.

47.

The Tanner Gantt Technique

We had another band practice the next week at Annie's.

"I wrote a new song," she said. "If you guys like it, then I'll teach it to everyone. It's called 'Thinking of You.'"

She slowly strummed some chords on her guitar, and then started singing:

"Thinking about you and what you're going through,
Thinking about you and what you have to do.

I know that every day is a challenge, just to
get through it,
    Sometimes I wonder, how do you do it?"

Was Annie singing about me?

"Late at night, I wonder what you're doin',
I wish I could make it better for you.
I know it's hard, to get through the night,
    There's got to be something I can do to make it
right."

Annie was totally singing about me!

"Looking for a place to rest, looking for
someplace safe,
    Somewhere warm and dry, and maybe a
friendly face.
    Looking for a home, to call your own."

I didn't know what that verse meant. I'd have to ask Annie.

"There's got to be a way—We can make it better,
To help you through your day—Let's all work together,
We've all got to reach out a hand—It's something we must do,
So, remember tonight, I'm thinking about you."

She strummed the last chord and looked up. Everybody clapped. I couldn't believe it. Annie had written a song about me. It was really cool and really embarrassing at the same time.

"Excellent song!" said Zeke.

"Annie, that was beautiful," said Capri.

"Wonderful melodic tonal structure and phrasing," said Abel (whatever that meant).

"Can we play it faster and louder?" asked Dog Hots.

"No, it's a slow song," said Annie. She looked over at me. "What'd you think, Tom?"

"Um . . . I . . . I don't know what to say. Thanks, Annie."

She looked confused. "Thanks?"

"Yeah, I appreciate it."

"What do you mean?"

"Well, I mean, it's nice for somebody to say that stuff and understand what it's like. . . . You wrote a song about me."

"*What?*" she said.

Capri laughed.

"It's not about you," said Annie. "It's about homeless people and what they go through."

I felt like The Stupidest, Dumbest, Most Idiotic, Biggest Ninnyhammer Dunderhead of All Time.

∘ ∘ ∘

I was pretty quiet when Zeke and I walked home afterward. I was feeling depressed, like Van Gogh. I mean, homeless people make me sad and everything, but I wish Annie's song had been about me.

Zeke tried to cheer me up.

"It *could* have been about you, T-Man. Except the part about not having a home and being alone. Maybe Annie will write a song about you someday."

"I don't think so," I said.

I left Zeke at his house and ended up at the park. It was dark, but I could see everything thanks to my night vision. Tanner Gantt wasn't on the swings that night.

I looked around to make sure no one was watching me and then I sat down on one of the swings. I didn't swing, exactly; I sort of sat there and moved back and forth a little.

I have to admit, I felt better afterward.

48.

Bat-Tom Rises

Ipracticed flying every night in my room. I was slowly getting better. One night in early November, I decided to fly around the house after everybody went to bed. I set my alarm for midnight. Quietly, I opened my bedroom door and changed into a bat. I flew down the hallway, down the stairs, around the living room, and into the kitchen.

My turns were okay and I did three perfect landings. I was taking one more spin through the kitchen when Emma came sneaking in the back door and I flew right into her hair.

She freaked out and started yelling.

"Help! Help!"

"Emma! It's me!" I yelled, but she didn't hear me because my voice isn't very loud when I'm a bat and she was screaming her head off. She tried to swat me with her purse, but she kept hitting herself in the head.

"Ow! Ow! Ow!" she yelled.

"Emma, stop! It's me!"

I finally got untangled and flew out of her hair. I hovered far enough away so she couldn't swat me.

"Emma! It's me! It's Tom! I'm a bat!"

She stared at me with her mouth open.

"You are the most disgusting thing I have ever seen! You are sooooo gross! Look at you. You've got big, bulging eyes and giant ears and fangy, little teeth!"

"Yeah, I know, Emma. I'm a bat. This is what bats look like."

She collapsed into a chair and moaned. "I have a bat for a brother. . . . My life just gets worse and worse every single day!"

I landed on the table. "Emma, *I'm* the Vam-Wolf-Zom, not *you*!"

"When did you learn to turn into a bat and fly?" she asked.

"Up at Gram's."

"How?"

I couldn't tell her about Martha Livingston. "I . . . I read a book."

"Is it called *How to Be a Bat and Fly*?"

"No. It's called *A Vampiric Education*."

She crossed her arms. "Where'd you get a book like that?"

"I found it on eBay."

"Okay, change back into yourself! This is too creepy! I don't want to talk to a bat!"

I turned back into me.

"Emma, *please* don't tell anybody I can turn into a bat and fly."

"Why would I tell anybody that my brother is even freakier than I thought?"

49.

Tree House Tears

Over the weeks before Thanksgiving, Zeke started taking banjo lessons on YouTube, Tanner Gantt got detention five times, Capri sang "Let it Go" at a band practice and we found out she can't sing at all and Annie made me tell her and she cried, Emma and Carrot Boy made up new nicknames for each other—Em-Em and Lukester, which are even worse than Emmers and Lukey— and my dad let Dog Hots use his old drum set. I read *A Vampiric Education* and found out that transforming into smoke is way harder than turning into a bat, and I still hadn't flown outside. But that was about to happen.

○ ○ ○

I was out in the backyard picking up Muffin's poop. For a small dog, Muffin poops a lot. I had just picked up Poop #4 when I heard a noise coming from our tree house. Mom and Dad built the tree house when Emma and I were little. Zeke and I used to play pirates and spaceship in it all the time. Emma used to go up there and write poetry when she was twelve and thought she was going to be the world's greatest poet.

"in a tree house"
by emma marks

here i am,
in a tree house
alone, above the world,

why?

Her poetry was worse than her flower paintings.

So, I was putting Muffin's poop into a bag when I heard somebody in the tree house crying.

"Emma?"

"Go away!" she yelled.

"What's the matter?"

"Nothing! . . . Go . . . away," she said. It didn't sound like her fake crying.

I climbed up the wooden ladder. Emma was sitting on the floor of the tree house next to her phone, wiping her eyes.

"Why are you crying?"

"I'm . . . I'm watching a sad movie."

"What movie?"

"Romeo and Juliet."

She's watched that movie a million times. I tried to watch it once because Annie said it was good, but I couldn't understand what anybody was saying.

Spoiler Alert: They both die in the end.

I looked down at Emma's phone. There was no movie playing.

"What's the matter?" I said.

"None of your business," she answered, wiping her nose on her sleeve. If I had done that, she would've said, "You are so disgusting!"

"What happened?" I asked.

She looked at me and her bottom lip started to tremble and then she blurted out, "Lucas is in love with Madison Debney!"

"Who's Madison Debney?"

"This new girl in Arts and Craft class! She

thinks she's all talented at making stuff and—and she has awesome dreadlocks and beautiful eyes and perfect cheekbones and the best smile and every guy at school is in love with her including Carrot Boy!"

I couldn't *believe* she called him Carrot Boy. That proved she was really mad. I was a little sorry they might break up. I was starting to think Carrot Boy was okay.

"How do you know he's in love with her?" I asked.

"He's been talking to her a lot at school."

"Why don't you just ask him about her?"

"You don't understand anything! Pari just called and she thinks she saw Madison at Luke's house tonight. I wish I could go spy on him and— WAIT!"

She got a crazy look in her eyes and pointed at me.

"You can go spy on him!"

"What?"

"Go turn into a bat and fly over to his house right now and see if Madison Debney is there!"

"I'm not gonna do that."

"Why not? Think of all the things I've done for you!"

I couldn't think of *anything* she'd done for me lately, except when she yelled at that guy at the Halloween store.

She looked at me with teary eyes and disgusting stuff coming out of her nose.

"Please, Tom?"

I knew I had to fly outside someday. If I didn't do it now, I might never do it. My landings were good and I never crashed anymore. I tried not to think of the videos of owls eating bats. Maybe those bats just didn't know to look out for owls? I couldn't remember ever seeing an owl in our town. I had seen hawks a couple of times. But I did have night vision, so I could be on the lookout, and if I flew fast and low to the ground they might not see me.

"Okay, Emma, I'll do it."

She gave me a hug, which never happens.

○ ○ ○

I knew I'd have to fly by Zeke's house and show him. He would kill me if I didn't. I called him to say I was flying over after I went to Carrot Boy's house.

"Excellent! I will be ready and waiting, Bat-Tom!" said Zeke.

I listened to see if it sounded like he was doing jumping jacks.

He wasn't.

"Okay, Zeke, be outside on your front lawn. Pretend you're looking at the stars or something."

Emma came into my bedroom. I opened my window and a breeze blew in.

"Okay, Tom, do it!"

I said, "Turn to bat. Bat, I shall be."

Bam!

I was a bat.

Emma shook her head. "That is . . . so . . . freaky."

I flew up to the windowsill. I looked out, very carefully, for owls or hawks or eagles. I didn't see any.

Emma said, "If you see Madison there, can you, like, fly in her hair and scratch her face?"

"No! I'm spying, I'm not attacking."

I took three deep breaths to get ready.

"Tom?"

"What?"

Emma lowered her voice. "Be careful."

I flapped my wings, lifted up off the sill, and flew outside.

50.

The Flight of the Bat-Tom

Why did I wait so long to do this?

Flying outside was a million times more fun than flying inside. I could go faster and higher and farther.

I went way up in the sky and looked down. I could see the whole city. It was like I was in an airplane, but *I was the airplane*. I stopped flapping my wings, held them straight out, and glided. A breeze pushed me along. The air was cool, the stars were out, I could see the almost full moon off in the distance.

Maybe being a Vam-Wolf-Zom was okay?

o o o

I flew over to Carrot Boy's house first. He was on his front lawn with a girl who looked exactly like Emma's description of Madison Debney. They were sitting on the grass, really close to each other. It didn't look good.

I landed on his roof. (It was a very good landing.) Carrot Boy was holding a box with a silver necklace in it. Madison gave him a hug. I felt bad for Emma. I cocked my ear to listen.

"Lucas, you are so sweet."

"No, I'm not."

"Yes, you are! You are such an awesome guy!"

"Well, you're pretty awesome too, Madison."

"Thanks."

"No, hey, thank *you* for making the necklace," said Carrot Boy. "Emma's gonna love it."

I could make out a little silver heart on a chain.

"I hope so," said Madison. "I think it's the best necklace I've ever made."

A motorcycle pulled up to the curb with a big, muscly guy who looked like Wolverine. Madison ran over and gave him a kiss that confirmed they were boyfriend and girlfriend.

"Later, Lucas!" said Madison as she climbed onto the back of the motorcycle.

Wolverine grunted and they roared off. Emma would be happy to hear all this. But first, I had to go to Zeke's house.

o o o

As I got closer, I could see Zeke standing on his front lawn with a pair of binoculars. When he saw me, he put the binoculars down and reached

into his back pants pockets. He pulled out two flashlights and turned them on. Then, he raised his arms straight up and started waving the flashlights back and forth, like workers do at airports for landing planes.

"You are cleared for landing, Bat-Tom!" he yelled.

"Shhh!" I yelled. But he couldn't hear me.

"Bat-Tom, flight twenty-seven approaching on runway three-thirty-five! You are good to land!"

I landed on the grass. Perfectly.

Zeke ran over. "Excellent landing!"

Normally he would have done jumping jacks for about five minutes, but he didn't. Martha Livingston was a good hypnotizer. Maybe someday I would be too.

I flew around Zeke's yard a few times, went way up in the sky, and then swooped back down. He watched me with his mouth hanging open.

"Okay, Zeke, I gotta go. I'll see you tomorrow!"

Zeke stood and raised the flashlights again.

"Bat-Tom is cleared for takeoff!"

Next stop: Annie's house, for a quick flyby.

○ ○ ○

I flew over our school, swooping down on the track and then back up again. I flew over the park, sailing across the tops of trees and Tanner Gantt's house. I didn't know he had a pool in his backyard, but when I got closer I saw there was no water in it. He had a big tree with a tire swing. I wondered if he ever sat in that swing.

I got to Annie's house and saw her in her bedroom on the second floor. I landed on her windowsill and peeked in. I was surprised that her room was messy. There were clothes all over the floor and the bed and her chair. Her bookshelf was crammed with books and little toys and figurines. On her wall she had a poster of that singer with the crazy hair and weird voice whose name I don't know how to pronounce.

Annie was sitting on her bed, next to a stuffed animal from one of those animated Japanese films she loves, strumming her guitar and singing. It was a song I hadn't heard before. She'd sing a little, then she'd stop and write down some words on a pad, and then sing again.

It sounded like a good song, even though it wasn't about me. I was just about to knock on the window when she sang the chorus:

"Listen to me, here is my song,
Listen to me, I'll sing it for free,
Listen to me, all night long."

I was figuring out a good harmony part for the song when Annie stopped singing and looked up at the window.

Right at me.

Could she see the brown bat sitting on her windowsill?

I froze.

Then, in the reflection of the window, I saw something else.

It was big, it was brown, and it was coming right at me.

I swiveled my head around. It was an owl, with wings spread and talons up, silently gliding directly toward me.

It looked hungry.

51.

The Owl and the Bat

Unless I did something fast, I was going to be this owl's dinner.

I flew off the windowsill and the owl missed me by an inch, slamming into the window. I flapped my wings as fast as I could. Maybe the owl had knocked himself out? I took a quick look behind me. He hadn't. He was coming after me.

Who knew owls could fly so quietly, and so fast?

Why didn't they teach us about owls in school?

Why didn't Martha Livingston give me a *How to Get Away from an Owl Who Wants to Eat You* lesson?

The owl got closer.

I decided to dive down to the ground and turn back into me. But the owl was so close I could feel the wind from his wings. He was going to get me before I could land on the ground and change. I had to do something fast.

Up ahead, I saw that the tree in Tanner Gantt's backyard had a small knothole. I could fly inside, where the owl couldn't get me.

I beat my wings as fast as I could, then pulled them in at the last moment and flew into the tiny entrance. The owl hovered right outside the hole. He tried to reach in with his talons, but I was just out of his grasp. He perched on a branch outside the hole, staring at me. He was going to sit there until I came out.

I couldn't turn into me because the hole was so tiny. Maybe if I yelled at the owl, he'd get scared and fly away.

"Hey! Get out of here! Go! Shoo!"

The owl blinked his big eyes a few times, but didn't move.

I imagined the owl taking me home to his nest.

"Hey, kids! Daddy's home! Look what I brought for dinner!"

"Yay! It's a bat!"

"He looks delicious, Daddy!"

"I want to eat his heart!"

"I want to eat his liver!"

"I want to eat his eyes!"

"Can we eat him while he's still alive, Daddy?"

"Yes, kids! That's the most nutritious way!"

It was going to be a long night in the knothole. I was hungry and tired. I fell asleep for a little bit, and when I woke up, the owl was gone. Maybe he was hiding, waiting to attack when I left the hole.

I slowly poked my bat head out. I didn't see him, so I flew down from the tree as fast as I could. Once I landed in the empty pool I said, "Turn to human. Human, I shall be!"

I turned back into me and looked up, spotting the owl on a branch just above the knothole. His eyes narrowed when he saw me. Then, he spread his wings and silently flew away.

o o o

I was walking toward the shallow end of the pool to climb out when I saw a skateboard with Rabbit Attack! stickers all over it. It was Zeke's. I knew Tanner Gantt stole it! I picked it up, climbed out of the pool, and heard a glass door slide open.

"Hey! What are you doing here, Marks!"

Tanner Gantt was standing on his back porch, holding a large, angry-looking dog on a leash.

"I'm getting Zeke's skateboard that you stole!" I said.

"I didn't steal it!"

"Then why is it here?"

"I bought it from Dennis Hannigan!"

Dennis Hannigan was a high school kid who made Tanner Gantt look like Winnie-the-Pooh. He was always stealing stuff.

The dog growled.

"You're trespassing, Marks! I'm calling the police!" Tanner shouted.

From inside, his mom yelled, "Tanner! Shut up! I'm trying to sleep!"

I jumped over the fence—in one leap, which felt kind of cool—and ran back to my house.

When I got home, I told Emma about Madison and Carrot Boy and the necklace. She started crying again.

"Lukester got me a necklace? He is so sweet! He is the best boyfriend in the world!"

"You know what else happened?" I said. "An owl almost ate me!"

"Oh," she said, brushing her hair.

"Did you hear what I said? I almost got eaten by an owl!"

"Right. Okay. But he didn't eat you."

"No! I wouldn't be here if he did!"

"So, what's the big deal? You're a Vam-Wolf-Zom. You can take care of an owl."

I started to explain, but decided it wasn't worth it.

Emma is the worst.

○ ○ ○

I gave Zeke's skateboard back to him at the bus stop the next day.

"Excellent! Thanks for getting this, T-Man!"

He was excited and for a second it looked like he was going to start doing jumping jacks, but he didn't. It was weird, I sort of missed him doing them.

We got on the bus and the first thing Annie said was, "You guys! Last night an owl almost broke my window!"

"Really?" I said. "What time is band practice tonight?"

Annie ignored my question. "I was working on a new song and this huge owl just banged into my window! I think he was trying to get a bird, or maybe it was bat."

"No, I don't think it could've been a bat," I said.

"Why not?" asked Annie.

Tanner Gantt got on the bus and for once I was glad.

"Hey!" said Zeke. "You stole my skateboard!"

"No, I didn't, Zimmer-Turd! I already told your trespassing friend, I bought it from Dennis Hannigan. 'Sides, it's a cheap, crappy board anyway. I only rode it once because it sucked." Then he turned to me. "Freak Face, if I ever see you on my property again, you are dead!"

52.

Spying

We had band practice that day after school. Dog Hots finally had a full drum set. Annie sang the new song that I'd heard when I watched her through the window, before I was almost killed by the owl.

When she got to the chorus I sang along with her and harmonized.

> *"Listen to me, here is my song,*
> *Listen to me, I'll sing it for free,*
> *Listen to me, all night long."*

That turned out to be a HUGE mistake.

Annie stopped playing her guitar. "How do you know that?"

"What?" I said, as innocently as I could.

"How did you know that song?"

"Uh . . . I just sort of . . . guessed?"

I couldn't tell her I'd been perched on her windowsill.

"How could you guess the words and the melody?" she asked suspiciously.

I shrugged. "I don't know. I must have heard you sing it before."

"That's impossible. I wrote it last night. There's no way you could know it, unless you heard me sing it. Wait, did you use your wolf-hearing to spy on me?"

"What? No!" (That was the truth.)

"Then how did you know it?!"

"I . . . read your mind?"

"Tell me!"

I didn't want to lie to her.

"Okay. Let me explain. . . . I learned how to turn into a bat and fly."

"About time!" said Dog Hots.

"So, I was flying by your house, and I was going to show you, and then I saw you in the window and—"

"You were looking in my window?!"

"Well, sort of—"

"You spied on me!"

"No! I wasn't spying. I just saw you sitting on your bed in your pajamas—"

"You spied on me in my bedroom!"

"*Technically*, I wasn't spying, because I'm not a spy. I saw you singing the song and—"

"YOU SPIED ON ME!"

"Annie, I was going to knock on the window, but that owl tried to kill me!"

"I don't care about that stupid owl!" yelled Annie.

"That owl could've taken me back to feed his baby owls! They were going to eat me alive!"

"Get out of here!" screeched Annie, going to her front door.

"Annie, come on, don't—"

She opened the door. "You are out of the band! And I don't want to talk to you ever again!"

"Annie, I didn't mean to—"

"GO!"

I walked out and she slammed the door.

"Don't slam the door!" yelled her mom from somewhere.

53.

Perks of Being a Werewolf

I was looking forward to getting away to Gram's for Thanksgiving (#5 on my Best Holiday list). Tanner Gantt kept saying he was going to call the police because I had trespassed, Capri was still mad at me for saying she didn't have a good voice, and Annie was even madder and wouldn't let me back in the band.

There was going to be a full moon on Thanksgiving night, so on the drive up to Gram's, Emma said, "Can we *please* eat dinner early, before you-know-who turns into you-know-what? I don't want to have to eat looking at his wolf face."

"Your brother has a very nice wolf face, Emma," said Mom.

"Mom, *nobody* has a nice wolf face. Except, maybe sometimes, in a movie. And we are not living in *that* movie. We are living in the Vam-Wolf-Zom movie!"

o o o

We always have Thanksgiving dinner early, before the sun goes down. I'm not a huge fan of turkey, but I love mashed potatoes and gravy and stuffing. I do not like broccoli and I never will. Pumpkin pie with homemade whipped cream is pretty good.

We didn't have any leftovers this year because I was zombie-starving and I had three servings and ate the rest of the turkey.

Dad was *not* happy about that.

"What?" he moaned. "No leftovers? No turkey sandwiches? No turkey salad? Turkey hash?" He looked sad.

"Okay!" said Mom, in her announcement voice. "Now, we are going around the table and everyone is going to say what they are thankful for."

Emma and I both groaned.

Mom started. "I am thankful that we are all here together."

"I'm thankful that we're healthy," said Gram.

Emma said, "I am thankful that Tom hasn't eaten any of us or sucked our blood . . . yet."

I smiled at her and said, "I'm thankful that Emma is going to college in two years."

"I am thankful that I don't have to do the dishes," said Dad.

Emma and I groaned again.

o o o

We have a Thanksgiving Rule: Mom, Gram, and Dad make the meal, and Emma and I do the dishes. While we're in the kitchen, working hard, washing the five hundred dishes and pots and pans and silverware, they're all by the cozy fireplace. Dad falls asleep on the sofa, Mom starts to read a book and falls asleep, and Gram puts on one of her old records and crochets. This time she was playing the Bob Dylan album Dad had brought her.

I was washing the big, disgusting gravy pan—which Emma always gets out of washing somehow—when the moon came up. I put the pan down as I started to change.

"Mom!" yelled Emma. "Tom isn't doing the dishes!"

"I'm turning into a werewolf!" I yelled.

"Stop yelling, I'm trying to sleep!" yelled Dad.

"Tom, when you're done changing, finish the dishes, please!" said Mom.

"Okay!" I said. "When I'm done, can I go run around the woods?"

"Yes!" said Mom.

"Can you all stop yelling so I can listen to my music!" yelled Gram.

∘ ∘ ∘

We finally finished the dishes. I raced out the back screen door and into the woods. The weather was cool and crisp and the fir trees smelled great. I ran up and down hills, jumped over fallen trees, and leapt off rocks, going really high in the air. I felt like I could run around forever. It's a pretty awesome feeling. It's one of the perks of being a werewolf.

After a while, I sat down on a log. I made a list, in my mind, of the good stuff and bad stuff that had happened over the past few months.

GOOD STUFF

1. I met another vampire: Martha Livingston.
2. I learned how to turn into a bat and fly.
3. Professor Beiersdorfer didn't turn Zeke and me into robots.
4. I got to dance with Annie.
5. I found out I have a great voice when I'm a werewolf.
6. Nobody recognized me when I went trick-or-treating and I got a ton of candy.

BAD STUFF

1. Tanner Gantt dressed up as me for Halloween.
2. I was almost Professor Beiersdorfer's pet bat.
3. Zeke and I came in last place for our science project.

4. I only have my great voice when I'm a werewolf.
5. An owl almost ate me.
6. Annie kicked me out of the band.
7. Annie hates me.

I got thirsty, so I trotted over to a stream and lapped up some cold, fresh water. While I was drinking, I heard a noise. Leaves crunching under somebody's feet. The sound got closer. I slowly raised my head and looked across the stream.

I could see it clearly in the moonlight. A gray face, white fur, the left blue eye surrounded by a dark circle. It was the werewolf that bit me. He was even bigger than I remembered.

Martha Livingston had told me to run away if I ever saw him again. He looked like he could easily leap over the stream and attack me. I couldn't outrun him, but I could turn into a bat and fly away. For once I was glad to be one-third vampire.

I quickly said, "Turn to bat —"

The wolf spoke.

"Good evening."

Acknowledgments

These people deserve a round of special thanks.

Jud Laghi, my agent, does all the important agenting things, so I can concentrate on writing.

Sally Morgridge is everything you want and need in an editor and continues to make these books better.

The gang at Holiday House who do all the massive behind-the-scenes work to get books out to you, the reader.

Mark Fearing, for the excellent illustrations.

John Simko, sharp-eyed copyeditor, who fixes all my mistakes.

Annette Banks, teacher, tutor, critic, sounding board, dance partner, nurse, Sherpa, confidante, who thankfully said "Yes" when I asked, "Will you marry me?"

Mom and Dad, always in my heart, whose generosity and support allowed me to write this book and the first one. (I won the Parent Lottery.)

Nancy and Alan, siblings supreme. (I won the Sibling Lottery, too.)

I'm lucky to have very good friends. "You've got to have friends to make the day last long and 2 get through this thing we call life."

Maryrose Wood for all the book world help. (Read her terrific books!)

Lord and Lady Marks for their very special help.

You, the person reading this right now. Keep reading, there are a lot of cool books out there!

And if you are STILL reading this, I am going to give you a sneak preview of the next book: Tom is going to meet the zombie who bit him . . .